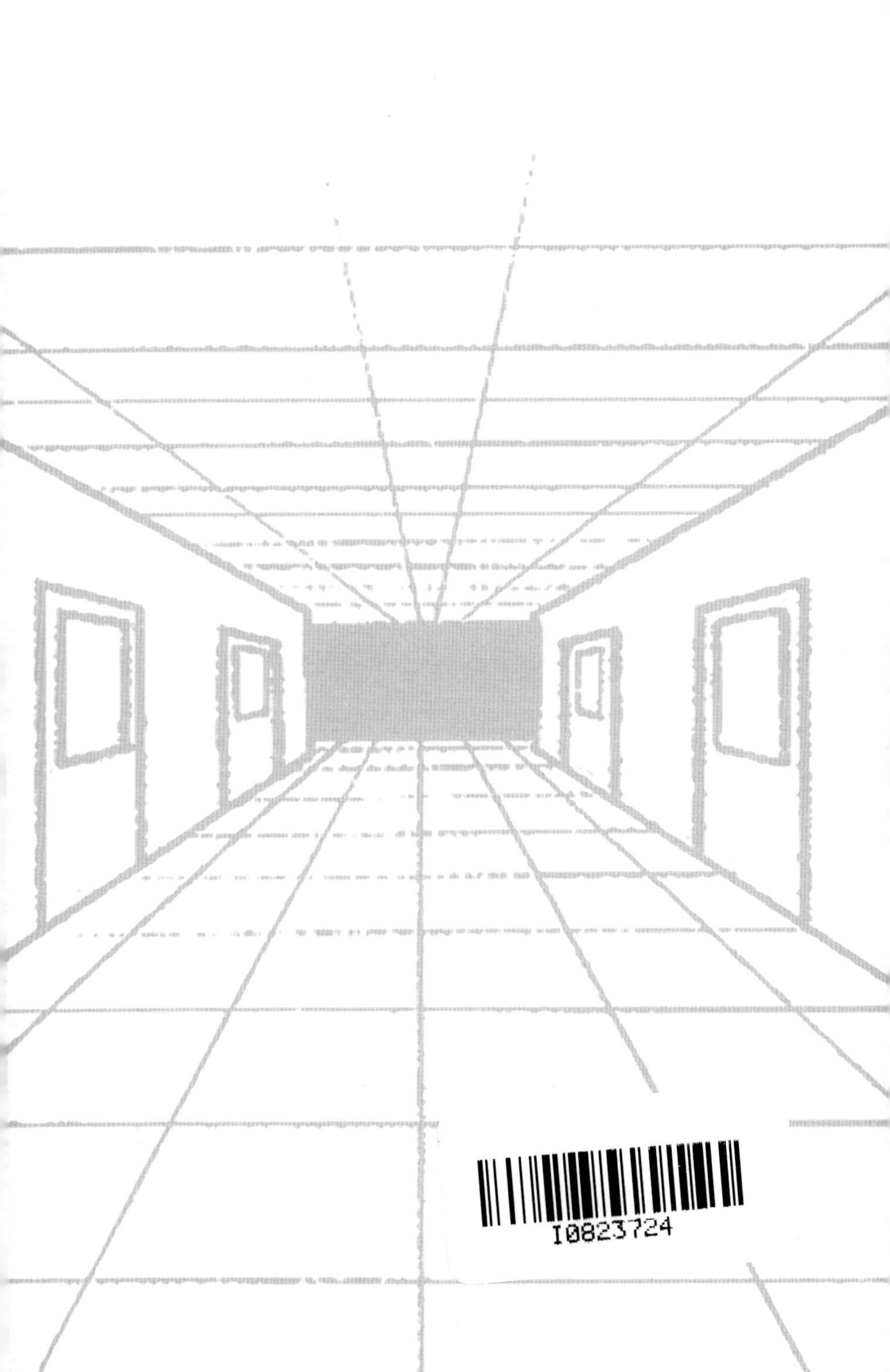

Born

HEATHER BIRRELL

Coach House Books, Toronto

first edition

Canada Council for the Arts Conseil des Arts du Canada

Canada

Published with the generous assistance of the Canada Council for the Arts and the Ontario Arts Council. Coach House Books also acknowledges the support of the Government of Canada through the Canada Book Fund and the Government of Ontario through the Ontario Book Publishing Tax Credit.

LIBRARY AND ARCHIVES CANADA CATALOGUING IN PUBLICATION

Title: Born / by Heather Birrell.
Names: Birrell, Heather, author
Description: First edition.
Identifiers: Canadiana (print) 20250113996 | Canadiana (ebook) 20250134411 | ISBN 9781552455005 (softcover) | ISBN 9781770568464 (EPUB) | ISBN 9781770568587 (PDF)
Subjects: LCGFT: Novels.
Classification: LCC PS8553.I792 B67 2025 | DDC C813/.54—dc23

Born is available as an ebook: ISBN 978 1 77056 846 4 (EPUB), ISBN 978 1 77056 858 7 (PDF)

Purchase of the print version of this book entitles you to a free digital copy. To claim your ebook of this title, please email sales@chbooks.com with proof of purchase. (Coach House Books reserves the right to terminate the free digital download offer at any time.)

And even when death is not a literal end, the tragic sense speaks to us of life's inevitable loss. Comedy, as tragedy's opposite number, offers a depiction of life in the key of hope.

– Ayad Akhtar, Author's Note, *The Who and the What*

Yes, there had been many times I called my daughters back to zip up their coats. All the same, I knew they would rather be cold and free.

– Deborah Levy, *Things I Don't Want To Know*

Elise feels a pressure in her bladder and bowels – this despite the fact she had run out for a quick pee right before the bell. She knew that to leave the students alone, even for a second, would mean at least partial mutiny. And she gets it, she does; she is not ignorant or unkind. They are sick of Shakespeare. It is the week before March Break. Lunch break was too short. Still, to fall behind at this point in the semester will mean too many pointed sidelong looks in the English office and she cannot bear it, not now, when she can already sense a swell of resentment building toward her. *Will you take the full leave? Do you know who will replace you?* There will be slack to be taken up, a new personality to integrate into the department's particular, peculiar ecosystem. Will the newcomer be game to contribute to the coffee fund? Will they spout wild, unconventional ideas about literature? Be overly authoritarian, rule-bound, patriarchal? Elise is scattered, and sometimes unfocused, but she knows the ropes, is a known quantity. And she is set to abandon them, teachers and students both. They are right to hate her a little.

She stares down at the pile of rubrics foregrounded on the desk, the slumped crowd sitting behind.

The assignment is to dramatize, somehow, the encounters they have had with Shakespeare and his work, and to examine their feelings – positive and negative – toward these encounters. Every year, a play, a rite of passage. Grade 9, *A Midsummer Night's Dream*; Grade 10, *Romeo and Juliet*; Grade 11, *Macbeth*; Grade 12 *Hamlet* or *King Lear* (or *Othello* if the teacher is brave). From comedy and hijinks to doomed love, to ambition and bloody murder, to ... all of it, really. Elise has told them she is looking for honesty, critical thinking, clear language, evidence that they have considered the source of their feelings, examined them with an eye to understanding them. Education buzzword: *metacognition*. And, in this case, Elise can see its worth. Literature should discomfit, she believes. But it should not alienate or exile its reader or audience. If Shakespeare has made them feel inept or stupid, the fault, surely, has been in the delivery of the material, not the work itself.

She knows they are more compelled by dystopian novels or novels-turned-films-turned-series, no matter how misshapen, derivative, pedestrian, or – she admits – occasionally genius these offspring of *The Handmaid's Tale* and *1984* may seem. They see themselves in the plucky teenaged protagonists, the chosen ones who fight their way through the obstacles their middle-aged capitalist, misogynist, racist, generally *-isty* overlords and ladies have plonked in the way of their actualization. And why shouldn't they?

She clears her throat, gives her head a shake. 'I know you're getting sick of Shakespeare, but I'm confident we can get through these presentations together if we focus, if we ... listen with our whole selves ... ' *Our whole selves?* She stands up, levering her body up awkwardly from the wheelie chair.

Still, she wonders where they will end up, those limber vessels of potential, at forty-six or fifty-three or seventy-one or eighty-five. She wonders about heroes, their long-term usefulness. If, like Olympic gymnasts past their prime, they find themselves fresh out of sponsorship deals, mired in the muck of everyday decisions about what to pack for lunch, whether to intervene in mild schoolyard disputes, how much is too much to pay for a new sofa and would bedbugs be an issue if we got it second-hand?

'We'll go first, Miss.' It is Faduma's group.

Elise sits back down, then wheels her chair to one of the empty student desks. She is amongst them now. There is a quietening. She notes Mark glancing over at her rubrics, her poised pen. Judge, jury, executioner.

'Okay, take a second to get prepared, and let me know when you're ready.' She wonders too: Where are the utopian novels? We disdain them in general, these mirages of perfection, and rightly so.

But maybe it's the perfection of possibility and not the possibility of perfection we should chase, the potential of working with what we have ... She types these half-formed notes into her phone where they float next to shopping lists, obscure movie titles, and the names of miraculous nutritional supplements people tell her about in playgrounds or at parties full of parents cross-eyed with fatigue.

What if ... What if a perfect world were premised on the impossibility *of a perfect world?* My god, she is blowing her own hormone-addled mind.

Faduma and her group have stood up from their seats and are gathered in a knot near the door, ready to make an entrance of sorts to the area in front of the blackboard that is their stage. *Life's but a poor player, strutting and fretting his hour upon the stage.*

Elise steels herself for another overwrought interpretation of a scene from *Macbeth,* when she feels a tidal pull in her abdomen; she exhales hard through her nostrils until it passes. Lady Macbeth has the sense to turn her wrath against her lady parts. No time for the petty concerns of procreation. *Come, you demons that tend on mortal thoughts, unsex me here.* Elise pats her protruding belly, sighs. Bit late for that.

Macbeth seems to be their favourite; there is a lot of blood and little in the subtle ways of love. Kindness and its offshoots are too quiet and unspectacular for Shakespeare. The gentler human qualities lack the technicolor propulsion of violence, of the inevitable bloodbath. A tragedy must end with a clear comeuppance, a death, preferably many. And a comedy? With marriage, the bonds of kinship tied up neatly, a monogamous march into happiness. Are there stories that live in the messy in-between? Of course. But will they hook a band of hormonal teenagers eager for freedom and fresh air? Doubtful.

'Now, Miss? Should we go now?'

She writes down their names – Faduma, Alison, Iryna, Soraya – and nods. Faduma and Soraya, the two hijabis, are the obvious leaders; she can see from their expressions that they are mildly irritated by the frivolity of their peers, who are staring out into the crowd between bouts of foot shuffling and hair flipping. Soraya nudges Iryna with her hip, shoots her a look that might be censure, might be stern encouragement. Elise sighs.

'Okay, everyone. I know you want to get through these and on to something new, but let's try for some respectful listening. Faduma's group, when you're ready, you may begin.'

Faduma nods. Their presentation is not from *Macbeth* as Elise had expected, but a quick recap from a scene in *A Midsummer Night's Dream*, the catfight between Helena and Hermia, translated into contemporary slang, followed by some observations about the enduring appeal of slut-shaming and the unfortunate business of competition for male attention within female friendships. Iryna isn't keen on the topic as she likes both boys and girls for lust purposes and futuristic fantasy novels for reading purposes. But she has gone along with the premise and has repeated her lines dispassionately in rehearsal. Alison is a surprisingly good actress, and has memorized her part with TikTok-style accuracy. They will do well if Soraya doesn't freeze, her social anxiety being selective and unpredictable.

They have only practised three times – well, 2.5 times actually, as they weren't all present every time, and Faduma still isn't sure Alison knows her lines or even understands the point of the assignment. Soraya knows her lines and has been at every practice but doesn't really get the point of much except chasing the marks she thinks will mean accolades from her parents, who speak constantly of her future role as a Somali-Canadian corporate lawyer. Faduma does get the point of the assignment; in fact, she often feels she has a window into Miss's brain, that she grasps the 'method in her madness'. Faduma understands that her teacher is trying to tease out their resistance to the Bard, spin it, express her solidarity with their objections, remind them of whatever deep and abiding connections they might have to Shakespeare's enduring and universal themes.

It's just that ... group work, amirite?

What Faduma means is that it rarely works the way it is supposed to, even if, as they are forever being reminded, it is rehearsal for the real world. In life, in whatever subsistence-level job they manage to secure in the post-secondary landscape, they will be forced to work with people very different from themselves. They will have to communicate clearly; there will be times when the work is not parceled out equitably, when one or another takes on a larger load, takes one, so to speak, *for the team*. There will always be dead weight. And: it is important to work with each group member's strengths. Because we all have our strengths.

Faduma glances at Alison, who is taking a selfie, her chin tipped upward and to the left, her eyes widened into an eerie gaze.

'When you're ready,' Miss says again.

Faduma pretends to scan the audience for Miss, but she has clocked her earlier; really, she is looking for Mark. He is sitting just behind the teacher, his chair tipped back slightly to make room for his long legs, his hoodie pulled forward so she cannot see his eyes. Maybe he will sleep through this. If only. Her gaze flicks over to the person sitting next to him; she can feel an unfriendly energy there. It is Shai-Anna, who meets Faduma's gaze, then narrows her eyes in what can only be construed as disdain.

It is after lunch when Maria arrives back at the school after a quick coffee run, but she decides not to go back to her office. She needs some time to re-enter without being known, to leave her therapist self behind for her straight-ahead administrative self. She ducks into an unlocked, empty computer lab, leaving the lights off, despite the fact that the classroom has no windows. She doesn't want to be found. Once she's booted up the computer, following the spinning discs and morphing screens like a lemming toward a cliff, the light from the monitor is enough. Her eyes adjust.

It is odd and somehow comforting, seeing the classroom like this. Without the camouflage and bustle of its students, it appears old and unkempt. There are cracks in the plaster, the paper that has been tacked over the bulletin boards as background is faded in sad patches, and no one has swept lately. The caretakers are short-staffed, the students seemingly unused to doing their own housekeeping. There is a circle of orange pop dried on the floor next to her. She presses her foot into it and her sneaker comes away with a satisfying *fwup*. It's like an institutional rec room, with all these portals to the outside world ready to glow up at the click of a button, grabbing for attention.

She allows herself to sink into the institutional hum of the school, with its hisses and clanks and groans, pressing her lower back into the chair, then sitting up straight and pushing her shoulders down in a stretch. Too much sitting – web-based training in Eye Motion Desensitization and Reprocessing for most of the morning – means that her body wants loose movement rather than this determined hunching. But in here she can avoid contact with the admin team, wait for the rest of the students to trickle their way out into the still bright light of the afternoon. She is a ghost.

Her body hurts from being sedentary, but there is a deeper, wilder hurt there too – it rips through her neck. She feels the music and the lights from the night before like a seizure – brief and all-consuming, body-rocking. A hand on her waist, moving up her rib cage, a dick pressed against her ass. People ask her all the time how she holds so much teenage angst and pain. And she has perfected her response. Clinical supervision. Her own unburdening and working through. Breathwork. Not true. Or only partly true. Drugs. Dancing. Sex in fumbled bursts. Inappropriate, as the students say, parroting their parents and teachers. *Inappropriate*. But necessary.

If people think it's impossible for one person to hold these disparate, warring things in their body and brain, they would be wrong. Because, my fucking god, the fucked-up things one person is capable of holding; she has seen them. She opens her student case files with a quick double click.

Anthony rides his skateboard toward the school, long strokes of sneakers against the street, hooded head looking up only to dodge the occasional kamikaze cyclist or stroller-pushing zombie mom. Why go back now, when he has been banished in no uncertain terms? Because it is the last place he saw Sam, and there is a possibility, remote but shining, that the Samantha he had encountered earlier, prone on her bedroom floor, is a fake, a clone designed to throw him off some cosmic scent. He will find Maria again – he messed it up this time, he knows. She will know what to say, who to call, how to put things back in the fucked-up order that made sense before. He understands this is all just wonky timing, some kind of weird and farcical mistaken-identity business. He thinks of Juliet waking up with a gasp beside Romeo. He yearns for a poverty-stricken apothecary to blame. Where is the law of Mantua when you need it most? He feels Sam's pulse, weak and fluttery under the fingers he pressed to the soft skin below her chin. He feels the wind against his own chin, the sound of his wheels' trucks as he flies across the school parking lot before flipping the board up and into his hands.

Faduma breathes deeply, into her diaphragm, and scans the classroom. First, a pivotal exchange in the original Elizabethan English.

'In this scene, Hermia believes Helena is out to get her man.' She nods toward Alison, who steps forward and sweeps her hand, thespian-like, toward the audience, who shift and snicker and … listen?

'O me! You juggler, you cankerblossom, You thief of love! What, have you come by night And stol'n my love's heart from him?' Alison lingers on *cankerblossom,* the hard *k* that catches in the throat, the irony of *blossom.*

Then Iryna, deadpan and slouching: 'Fie, fie, you counterfeit, you puppet, you!' She hesitates for just long enough before pronouncing *puppet.* And it gets a laugh, a pretty big one considering the circumstance.

Then the PA crackles and Principal Jackson speaks. 'We are in lockdown. I repeat, we are now in lockdown.'

Maria always winces at Sharon's voice when it comes on over the PA. Chirpy middle management; it is the kind of demented cheerfulness that makes her gag. Still, as a principal, Sharon's not the worst Maria has encountered. A little too law-and-order for her liking, but usually has the kids' best interests at heart. But the chirping? It's almost unforgivable. It takes Maria a moment to register what Sharon is saying.

A lockdown. She is calling a lockdown. Likely not a drill, although Maria wouldn't put it past her to try an impromptu dry run of sorts; Sharon is an administrator who believes it is possible to be prepared. But if it is the real thing? It's normal for Maria to attribute trouble to the students she sees: normal and not unfounded. They are at the root of a lot of trouble; they do not 'get into' trouble, trouble lives inside of them rent-free. Despite their earlier encounter, Anthony does not come immediately to mind; she runs through a shortlist before his name surfaces. But once her mind alights upon him, it stops. And she knows. Sweet, stupid boy, she thinks. Why couldn't you stay away?

CRAMP

ELISE

I get Jessica and Bryce to close the window blinds and Mohammed to move some of the desks so we can all sit against the walls, out of sight of the 'intruder,' who is still snuggled in quotation marks, because who knows if this is real or a drill, something ordered by the administration and the police department, or a real threat to our safety?

'Miss, is this a drill?'

'Shh,' I say, and shake my head no, because I suspect it is but don't really know, and although they are not, as a rule, contrary or boisterous, I know a whiff of authenticity will make them more meek, compliant. And there are public shamings for those who do not follow proper protocol during a lockdown drill – a lecture over the PA system that reports the room numbers of offending classes, then lists their deviations. My baby kicks once inside me; there is not much room to be had these days, and it annoys her.

I ask Mark to cover the windows on the doors with the chart paper we have used to explore (Explode! I like to say. Let's not just explore, let's explode these themes! See what interesting shards break free!) *Othello*'s most pressing questions. We must not allow the shooter any visual access to our space. When Mark tapes up the sheets, we are all faced with our own colourful mind maps. I have asked them to imagine various scenarios and they have responded with their own wild teenage notions and priorities, drawn lines and clouds and little squiggly arrows to show how their opinions connect and conflict. The words are written in bright rainbow shades, scrawled in diagonals or neatly penned. *WTF – of course I would be mad if I thought my girlfriend cheated!!! My parents would NEVER let me marry someone outside of my culture. Don't listen to your parents – mix it up, baby! Bros before hos.*

I love teaching literature because it demands we flex our emotional intelligence, see beyond ourselves, accept the maddening, mouldering complexities of our fellow humans. And I do think the best of it is about people, rather than 'issues.' But this is not the way the bureaucrats and purse-string holders operate. They need a word or event to revile and a published, pristine stance to venerate, or they are not happy. But art has never fit easily into our data-driven schemes; it is unquantifiable, not easily standardized. Right? Right.

Fuck that, I wish a superintendent could see us *now*, how authentically engaged we are in the best project-based learning *ever*. It is, by necessity, student-centred and experiential.

It's true that I was excited about the possibilities of *Othello*. So many contemporary connections regarding race, gender relations, power and its relentless pursuit, domestic abuse! I thought, I really did, that I was someone who could make it happen – make the Bard relevant despite his dead white maleness, defeat the naysayers who somehow believe today's youth incapable, unable to fathom Shakespeare's language or wisdom. We must find ways to *connect*, they say, and they speak as if teachers are nothing but sophisticated modems and students just ports to be plugged into. What other demographic is so consistently vilified and sexualized and commercialized and infantilized? Hey, teacher, leave them kids alone! But the students are mandated, required by law, to be here. And I am required to teach them. And it is true, it is, that they pay me relatively well, and I get these holidays that make regular nine-to-fivers fizz with vitriol.

And if my students have eaten enough for breakfast, if I catch them on a good day, they might take some of these ideas, allow them access like earworms, and the ideas might burrow through and nest somewhere ...

And what? They will be changed? *Jesus*. Who has been watching too many triumphant teacher movies? What I'm trying to say is that there is very little choice here for us, so maybe I can control a little and maybe that little will not be a bad thing. What people fail to mention about teaching in a public school is that it is at root an anti-intellectual venture, designed to keep you busy with forms and labyrinthine procedures, platforms that lead to platforms that land on wobbly platforms that spit out median marks and assessments of learning skills, attempting always to make hard data out of fleshy, chaotic human beings. If there are moments of epiphany? Of true learning? How to describe these moments without coming across as saccharine, self-aggrandizing? They are often so incremental as to seem insignificant, comical in their slow waddle toward revelation.

Those who can, do; those who can't, waddle toward revelation.

And now we are locked down together. Fewer choices still.

But it is a drill the students take in stride; most of them have done it since grade school. If they think about the ramifications of the procedure, they seldom let on. If this is real, it will become a story or a boast; if it is not, an annoyance, a grievance to be aired.

Everybody is sitting where they should except Shai-Anna, who is lounging on my wheelie desk chair, her back against the blackboard.

'On the floor,' I mouth to her.

'The floor is nasty,' she says, curling her lip.

'Shh,' I say emphatically, and also too loudly. The baby kicks again. 'Sit,' I mouth, my eyes wide and intense.

She rolls her eyes and lowers herself to the floor, where she hovers in a crouch. Then she waddles over to the other side of my desk and pulls down an abandoned accounting textbook. She slides it under her bum and settles in, smug. I shake my head, but I am letting her have her clever point.

Strange how the more real this school-based (mostly American, it must be said) violence becomes through newscasts and internet think pieces, the more buried the fear becomes, the more blasé the reaction to these drills, which belong in wartime, in a different time entirely.

My job is to keep the kids quiet and out of sight of a possible shooter. A shooter! My colleague Steph, who teaches math, mostly to Grade 9s, has a line: *I didn't sign up for this*. She proclaims this at least three times a day, gesturing toward an unruly student, a broken piece of chalk, a squashed french fry in the hallway, a memo that has landed in her inbox. Ha! I didn't sign up for this. My baby kicks in agreement and I place my hand against what I think is her bum. You didn't sign up for this, I think. But none of us do.

I scan the classroom. Do a quick head count. Twenty-seven. I check the attendance list: twenty-eight. Shit. I made a mistake, or no, I know, I let Samara go to the bathroom before they called the lockdown. So now she is stuck. Or maybe in another classroom? The instructions for if you are caught in the can are pathetic. Lock the stall and crouch on the seat so that anyone entering *will not know you are there.* I am not religious, or only nominally so, but I say a little prayer for her. She is more concerned with her eyeliner than opening a book, but I wish her no harm.

The baby kicks again – and this is not even her active time! – then repositions in a way I find intensely uncomfortable. I realize I am squatting in what is possibly an undignified manner. I am pleased to be wearing a calf-length cotton jersey dress; stretchy and blue, it drapes over my great mountain of a belly to fall semi-modestly into my lap. I scan the students to see if anyone is catching this pregnant-lady spectacle. Josh is tossing a roll of masking tape high into the air, but quietly, with a casual skill I admire. Camila is performing some contortion that might be yoga, might be TikTok dare. There are whispers everywhere, a susurration born of boredom and mild fear. They are not interested in me.

Still, I am well into the third trimester and certain ways of moving in the world have become impossible. I place my hands on the floor behind me – which is, I agree, nasty – and lower my ass down. Then I cross my legs as if ready to meditate or sit still for storytime, which is not a bad way to think about getting through a lockdown, considering the unknowns, the great Pause button that has been pushed by the Authorities.

It is forbidden to use cellphones during a lockdown. Why? Because it could *interfere with police investigations.* About two-thirds of my students are absorbed in their phones, thumbs stroking, eyes flicking and widening like senior citizens entranced by the lucky shapes that spin inside a slot machine. Some do this in what they imagine is a surreptitious manner.

They are aware of the rule. Are they clogging the internet funnels? Dropping social media bread crumbs, providing clues to the intruder as to the target's whereabouts? It is a risk they are willing to take. Or just what they *do*; not so much risk as a matter of course. Fate?

These things, these shootings, have really happened, I know. To lambs, little children less knowing than the sweet, strident beings gathered around me. Still, I have trouble believing it. I am both terrified of and somehow nonplussed by the thing itself, the gun. I have seen it so many times on screens, it seems impossible that it could occur, IRL, as my students would say, without the distance a camera creates.

I wonder what they are feeling. I scan them, looking for signs of anxiety, something that will betray a nervousness, a bravado born of terror. Two students appear to be sleeping. Ryan meets my eye, then quickly looks away. He is younger than the rest, trying to fast-track through to a career in chemical engineering. He has told me exactly where he will end up, engineering his own life as far as humanly possible. This lockdown is not in the plan. I smile at him in what I hope is a reassuring manner but am overtaken by a cramp that begins in my hip flexors and somehow travels, undulating, to my belly button. I have managed to grimace at perhaps my most vulnerable student. I am not a good role model. I check my watch. It has been eleven minutes since they called it and I have not yet heard any encouraging boss-lady heel clicks or stealthy thumps of police officers checking to see that we are settled and compliant, hiding from harm. So it is possible this is real. I allow myself to think about this.

There is a threat in the school. He possibly has a gun. (Or she? No, not a she, it is never a she. Why? When we have so much more to disgruntle us? Oh, right. Because we are taught to turn the anger onto ourselves or each other.) He is finding his way around the school like a predator, eyes narrowed, steps careful and slow. He is wearing good sneakers, expensive, the ones designed to impress on the basketball court. He's white and he bears a grudge. There are many role models available to him.

There are many role models available to me too – mostly dead. Quick-thinking but doomed, they placed themselves bravely in the shooter's path to protect their students. They are the patron saints of self-sacrificing teachers everywhere, posthumously honoured for flinging themselves in front of the kindergartener or shielding a teen by confusing the shooter with sly distractions. Martyrs to the cause.

You will forgive me if, in these moments, my thinking tends toward the baroque and superstitious. It is not safe, really, to mention mommy brain – the rush of blood to the fetus, the forgetfulness and dropsies, the bloat of emotion – because who wants to give the world more ammunition for suggesting our female organs make us incompetent? But there are days when it is difficult to separate from the soupy mess of hormones that is this human-making machine.

So I will say this now: I care for my students; there are some I even adore in certain moments, but if ever I say I love them? It is because they have adhered to our agreement and fulfilled their role as learners. They have demonstrated a skill, questioned a text, finally learned and applied the difference between *there, their,* and *they're.* They have made me laugh. For instance, a student once used the following as a complex thesis statement for an argumentative essay: *There is something fundamentally both miraculous and superdisgusting about dental floss.* My love for my students is a love that inflates my own sense of competence in this, my chosen profession.

But do I *love* them, the way I do my own flesh and blood, this creature growing inside me, my seven-year-old son at home, my husband? Would I leap to their aid if the shooter burst through that door, guns ablaze?

No. I would save myself. I would save my baby. And if that makes me cowardly and unworthy, so be it. I did not sign up for this.

ANTHONY

I can't find Maria anywhere. Her office door is locked and there is no fluorescent light seeping out from under it. It's not like her to leave mid-afternoon. Usually, she puts Post-its with smiley faces on her door when she ducks out for a bathroom break. So where is she now?

I duck into the caretaker's closet when I hear them call the lockdown.

The closet is long and deep and in the guts of it there are stacks of brown paper towels and unlabelled spray bottles full of fluorescent pink and dull green liquids. I am pretty sure that if I pushed the packages and the shelving unit aside, I would find the entrance to the lava-covered mountains of Mordor or the snowy woods of Narnia, but I don't have the strength right now, plus I would never want to go on that kind of quest without Sam. At first, I am scared. I look around for recycling bins or old printers I could use to barricade the door. I try not to breathe. I don't want the shooter to find me. But then it comes to me that in the eyes of the school, in the eyes of the authorities, I am the problem, the threat, the intruder. I need to talk to Maria. I didn't explain properly what had happened, what spirit had moved me to stay close to the knife, to have it, as they say, *on my person*.

Sam would think this was *high*-larious, that they actually called a lockdown for *me*. What should I do? If I come out of the closet – ha! – as the knife-wielding wannabe killer that I am, there will be too many eyes on me, the eyeball-jelly sort and the beady electronic sort, and I don't think I can bear that right now. I need time to think of a plan. I will wait until everyone is properly locked down. So much noise now. It's not terrified noise; there is no terror. They still think it's a drill; they think I'm a drill. And they're wrong. I am not a drill. Sam is not a drill. What we *feel*? What we *are*? It's real. They can't Snapchat us out of existence.

My leg is cramping because I've scrunched myself behind some kind of industrial floor cleaner that looks like the vacuum cleaner in *Teletubbies*. Sam and I binge-watched episodes once when we were high and that squat blue thing with the squinched-up elephant nose made her literally piss her pants laughing. I'm peeing, she said, between these gaspy breaths, I'm *actually* peeing. She went home in a pair of my jeans with her scarf threaded through the belt loops to keep them from falling down over her skinny hips. I look like a cross between Drake and a fucking construction foreman, she said. I'd still do you, I told her. I know, she said. I'm shit-hot like that.

I can still hear footsteps in the hallway – soft-soled and unalarmed. It occurs to me that it is one of the caretakers. Maybe the short white one who always smells a bit boozy? Element of creepazoid but basically harmless. *Maybe, if you don't have breasts,* says Sam. True dat, sister, I whisper, which makes her laugh. The footsteps come closer. The closet door opens and a shaft of institutional light falls across the floor. I think my sneaker is showing. I concentrate on keeping my foot very still. I am holding my breath and then not – I let it leak out slowly through my nostrils. When I breathe in again, I can smell the boozy caretaker. *Cheap hooch,* says Sam. *It's the Newfie.* Racist, I reply, which makes her crack up. The caretaker lets out a sigh. Like his job's so hard. He turns out the light and closes the door. I listen hard for the jangle of keys. I am fucked if he locks me in here. My bones might be excavated hundreds of years from now. I'd be fleshless behind the still intact bulk bottles of ammonia. But he doesn't lock it. I hear him shuffling away.

I am so fucking tired. I am tired of my own self. Where are you, Sam? Please don't leave me, okay? I know that life is ultra-shit for both of us right now, but if we ever get out of this and actually manage to find a place in the world, I'd really love it if you could keep sending me abusive texts and pointing out my blackheads.

There's a reason to keep living! It's possible that once we cross over into adulthood, we will have fewer zits! Downside: if we're 'lucky' we will have 'real' jobs.

Go to the paper room, Ant. Get there now. You fucked up by telling that cunty counsellor about your sweet little obsessions, but you can make it better now. Go somewhere far away from the people – so they know you are not a danger to society. Charge your phone and put on some boring science podcast. Try to sleep. That's what I'm doing. Trying to sleep until they decide what to do with me.

They? Who's they?

I dunno. The Architects of the Universe.

I thought you were an atheist.

I am, but it's easier to attribute the whims of fate to beings greater than myself that accept the general randomness and rude irrationalism of the universe.

OMG, you're dumb.

Yep. And *I'm in a coma. Go to the Paper Place.*

Okay, on it.

I pull myself up to standing and my foot immediately cramps. I stumble and come close to bringing the whole shelving structure down on top of me. But then I do this little moonwalk move and save myself. I stop for a minute until my foot feels better, then shuffle over to the door and press my ear to it. Like a spy.

I open the door and do a quick one-two whip of my head.

Coast is clear.

You are catching all the Ls right now.

Yes, but this is necessary. This is some real shit.

Go to the Paper Place, Ant. Just get there.

I slip my knapsack on both shoulders and step out into the hallway. It smells like sweat and old curry. The wall I am facing is painted with graffiti-style positive affirmations. *Every thought we think is creating our future.* Oh, great. The words are curving around the crest of a wave – for a moment I imagine getting lost in that wave.

Going under. Then Sam gives me a nudge and I begin inching my way along the wall toward the staircase.

So stealthy.

Fuck off, Sam, I'm trying. A walkie-talkie crackles into my consciousness. *South entrance clear,* comes the voice. I recognize the voice of the newest hall monitor. He's very tall, wears too much cologne, and adjusts his balls a lot when he thinks no one's looking. Or maybe he knows people are looking? What's his name again?

Ant? Focus. He's looking for you, you know.

Right. It is me they are hunting. I am the hunted. Jesus fucking Christ. I contemplate doubling back to the lockers next to the caretaking closet. I could shut myself in. I could suffocate.

Go to the Paper Place, Ant. Sam makes a spooky ghost voice, breathy, deep, and male.

And that makes me laugh because I know she is trying for Hamlet Sr. at the part where he's convincing Hamlet Jr. to get revenge. *Swear.* We memorized it because it sounded so D&D and had all this awesome stuff about purgatory.

> I could a tale unfold whose lightest word
> Would harrow up thy soul, freeze thy young blood,
> Make thy two eyes, like stars, start from their spheres,
> Thy knotted and combinèd locks to part
> And each particular hair to stand on end,
> Like quills upon the fearful porpentine.

Fearful porpentine. Sam whispers. *Porpentine, porpentine, porpentine.* Then I hear the walkie-talkie static again, but it is retreating, moving toward the junior gym and pool – places me and Sam never go – so I just make a break for it, quick and fleet-footed, up the stairs and through the English hallway. My breath comes in pants, but I contain it – two long steps at a time, a pause – and I am there.

ELISE

Someone in the corner is sniffling. It is Faduma. I watch her lift the corner of her hijab to dab at the snot in the divot under her nose. There are tissues on my desk. My son, Joey, builds incredible structures out of tissue boxes. Nose-wipe towers, he calls them. I shuffle over and carefully tip the tissue box off the edge so that it lands softly in my cupped hands. Then I begin a slow backward bum shuffle in Faduma's direction. She is crying, I can tell. Three more bum pushes. I swing my legs around and push my body in next to hers.

'Hi, Miss,' she mouths.

'Hi,' I mouth back, and hold out the box.

'Is this for real?' She takes the box from me and pulls out one, then two of the cheap, one-ply institutional squares.

I shrug. I know better than to lie to her. *Maybe,* I say with my eyes. Her eyes fill again and she nods.

I reach my arm out to embrace her, but the movement incites another cramp, this one with its node in my deepest pelvis. It intensifies, then branches out like a star into every nook and corner of my abdomen. I make a sound like a snake, the air escaping between my clenched teeth.

'Careful, Miss,' she says. 'You're pregnant.'

People keep telling me this. As if there is anything they could say that could be more blatant and instructive than my own body's workings.

'Not much longer,' I say. I jerk my head toward the clock.

Faduma's eyes widen. 'You mean?' she whispers. She reaches her hand out toward my belly and I put my own hand over hers so that she is sandwiched between me and my baby.

'No, not that.' I smile. 'The lockdown. I'm sure it will be lifted soon.' Her lips form an *oh* of acknowledgement, then an *ah* of surprise as the baby nudges us both. I am suddenly very hot but know it would be rude to lean away from this girl I have so recently singled out for attention. My armpits are clammy, and oh, I'd like to be lying in my own bed, curled on my side, a pillow clamped between my cumbersome thighs.

'Shh,' I say curtly, because I can feel the group on the opposite wall start to hum with impatience.

Shushing, constant overloud shushing, is said to calm a newborn. It approximates the white noise of the womb, helps the poor, suddenly-outside being feel held and surrounded and safely inside again. But I remember being told never to shush a high school classroom. Teenagers do not register the subtle sound of the sea. They respond to direct, positive command. They listen to compelling pop-culture authority, not to their mothers. Still, it has not stopped me from shushing intermittently when they are far gone in their own worlds. Sometimes, in these situations, they gaze at me benignly, as if I am a faraway airplane that has entered their field of vision. No, as if I am a person on that plane, waving.

There are moments when I feel this remove as a comfort – the knowledge that I play such a small part in their day-to-day. Peer-involved is what they are. And yet our admin team reminds us in every staff meeting of the pull we exert on them, our influence and importance, our vital role in ensuring not only that they graduate but that they avoid dangerous street drugs, suicide, self-cutting, online bullying.

And now here we are. Barricaded in a classroom. Hunkered down out of sight of the shooter. Quiet. Sort of.

'Quiet,' I mouth to the clump of girls to my left, leaning up against the poetry anthology cabinets. They turn toward me and smile sweetly. But sweetly like the pseudo-sugar in pink packets that always leaves me feeling jangly and unsatisfied. I look at the clock, then check my watch. Thirty-three minutes. It is not a drill.

ANTHONY

It makes me giddy to see the endless trench of hallway empty of kids. It is so quiet. Everyone so contained, so *compliant.* I try out walking past the classrooms slowly, powerfully. Is it wrong to say something in me is thrilling at my might? So many souls shut away in these shitty, institutional pods.

Whoa, Ant.

I know, right?

It's not so much the sentiment, it's the expression. Super-extra. Like you're on emo steroids or something. Getting all 'Check out my fatal flaw.'

You're right. And there is a lonely pull to whatever this feeling is – a messed-up teen version of Ambition. I pass room 105, room 107. I slow down. There is something different about room 108: an ... energy.

You've got to be fucking kidding me.

No, it's true, Sam. There's *something* there. Something about those people. Maybe they are *our* people?

They are not our people.

The thing is? What I'm realizing? I'd rather be in there with them. In the pathetic soul-sucking pods. Hiding from someone like me. I wonder if maybe it is not too late. I could say I was in the washroom or I was too scared to come out of the cafeteria. I could just knock, right? Tell them there's been a misunderstanding?

Ant? You are hella emotionally dysregulated right now. Just sayin'.

I stop in front of room 108 and consider my next move. I need some time to think. It was Sam who gave me the key to the Paper Place and showed me the spot behind the stacks, how you could crawl in there and for a while it could be your fortress. You could always get into the staff room and the photocopy room, no problem. But the paper room was locked, and even teachers had to call a caretaker with a shackle full of keys to open it. So I'm still not sure where she got the key or why she thought it might be okay to give it to me. But she did. And I have it in my pocket now. I feel it when I slide my way down the door of 108, my back up against it. The key presses into my butt as if to remind me. Like I need reminding.

I want to be enclosed. I am ready to be locked up, out of the way, out of harm's way, out of my own harming way.

I see it clearly.

It is less like a movie than a hyperrealistic animation that comes to life for a few seconds in the dark theatre of my brain. There is blood everywhere. It is always a knife. And I am not merciful. It is not something I can control. The knife is a butcher knife. Or a Swiss Army knife. Or the type of short, sharp knife my mother uses to peel vegetables – a potato or turnip pinched in her other hand. I don't know why I stab them. I just know that I have to. There is blood of course. And horror. I don't invite the thoughts; they just burst like gremlins into my mind's eye – uninvited, unbidden.

But maybe not unexpected, right? I mean, we all know about triggers. Everyone is always getting fucking triggered. Just whisper the word *rape* and every girl and her BFF is wailing about some shit they went through billions of years ago or at last week's excuse for a party. And I think, *really?* That's what you call triggering? I'll show you triggering, motherfucker. Show me anything remotely related to cutting and I'll show you a guy getting the shit triggered out of him. You don't even need to show it to me. You can merely reference it in passing. Like: What the fuck, fam, why didn't you get me a slice? Or: Wanna cut class next period? You could just be a pair of scissors existing innocently on a teacher's desk, not even doing any dangerous pointing, not accusing anyone or anything. You could be Macbeth. You could be slicing butter with a crappy plastic serrated thing. You know there's a cologne called Axe? Yeah, that. Nail clippers. The paper cutter. Steak knives and bread knives and medieval swords.

And it doesn't escape me that I am fucking up the stereotype. I know it should be guns. Disaffected. Teenaged. Male. You know that I'm white too, right? And a loner? Not gang-involved. I like to wear black, but not always. So, yeah. It should be a gun, right? Something automatic and efficient. I should be thinking machinery of death, not getting all 'Is this a dagger I see before me?' But whatever, I've never been good at fitting in; no reason my murderous tendencies should be up to code.

OhmiGAWD, Ant. Shut. Up.

I don't want it, I tell Sam. This is not what I want. Still, the knife in my backpack is telling a different story. And doesn't your own brain know what you *really* want? I mean, in its depths, in what they call the subconscious, those hidden disgusting parts of yourself? Can you blame me if lately I've been thinking the only way to get rid of the thoughts might be to actually see them through? Like, to *do* them?

ELISE

There is a noise in the hallway. A door opening and closing. Samara? Would she risk a return from the bathroom? Or maybe it is a drill? A cop coming to check that our window coverings are complete? That we are not using this time to play poker or shout obscenities out the windows? But the steps are too tentative. The students hear them now too. They are listening like me.

We are holding our collective breath.

My baby rolls and it is painful, visible through my blue dress. Not a large movement. She's too big for that; it's tight in there. Be still, I will her.

The person outside does not try the door. But we all hear a body leaning up against it, then sliding downward, the door shuddering with movement. I have both hands on my belly now. I am holding on to her, my future. My students have not yet exhaled. They are looking toward me. I look back at them, try to meet each and every set of eyes through the thicket of desks and chairs.

Okay, I do love them. But still, I did not sign up for this.

MARIA

It is doubtful anyone will even bother with this computer lab. I checked the door was locked when I closed it behind me. I am safe from the demands of the higher-ups, safe from the intruder. The intruder? I shake my head, resist the urge to hunker down on the floor as I have in countless drills. I am a ghost. I double-click on Anthony's file, open my notes.

I had tried using CBT with him, introduced it in one of our last sessions together.

'I know it sounds dumb,' I said. 'I do. But it's just a way of re-ordering your thoughts, getting some perspective.'

He didn't even nod, just looked into my eyes and gave what I thought might be an eyebrow twitch of assent. I found my work-sheets and handed him a copy. He looked over the chart quickly and barely suppressed a snort. I was happy with that, though, the attempt at suppression. He was trying to please me; he didn't think I was a total dick.

'So we take one of your most upsetting or disturbing thoughts. That's where we start.' I pointed to the first column. It is a stretch for me, turning a landscape of fear and pain into a spreadsheet, lining up feelings like kindergarten children against a wall. But it is where we have found ourselves, in the absence of exorcisms and psychedelics, in the presence of peer-reviewed studies, of data. And I know that more than any other, this medicine is faith-based. I must also believe.

Anthony nodded.

'Can you tell me about the thought?' I used a gentle tone. 'Just try to describe it.'

'I'm stabbing someone,' Anthony said quietly.

I nodded. I was doing my therapist face. Neutral, open, expectant – but not too judgy. Not judgy at all. 'Okay,' I said. 'Is that all?'

'I can't stop stabbing them. And the blood is everywhere.'

He began to cry and I let him. I did not pause or lean over the desk to helpfully pass the Kleenex box. I stayed still and silent, listening.

'I don't want to do it. I don't want to see it, but it's there. Like a dream, only worse. Something that's somehow moved into my brain.'

He had squeezed his eyes shut, as if to squeeze the image out. And now his hands were clamped around his head, also squeezing. It was time to bring him back.

'Anthony, open your eyes. It's okay. Where were you when you had this thought?'

He mumbled something toward the floor.

'I'll write this first one out for you if you like. We're not really supposed to do it this way; you're supposed to take ownership of it from the get-go and all that, but what the hell, right?'

He was watching me like he knew I was making a show of bending the rules to get him onside. He was right. I wanted him onside. He nodded.

'So.' I sat up straighter. 'Where were you when this thought happened?'

'Here,' he said.

'Okay, you were here. You mean at school?'

'No, in your office.'

'Okay, in Maria's office.' I wrote it down in big blocky letters. MARIA'S OFFICE.

'How did the thought make you feel?'

He spoke more clearly this time but did not lift his head. 'Scared. Really fucking scared. Ashamed. Pukey.'

'Go on.'

'You were there.'

'Was I? Anthony, were you stabbing me?'

He nodded.

How should I record this? *stabbing maria*, I wrote, in lower case this time. It would make a good band name. The Stabbing Marias. I had flipped the meaning – as a coping mechanism maybe? Who was the stabber? Interesting.

I took a deep breath, but as quietly as possible. Breathing calms the nervous system. Breathing is also medicine. 'Okay, got it. On a scale of one to ten, how would you rate the strength of your emotion?'

Anthony shrugged.

I wrote ten. 'And what was your follow-up thought after having this thought? The thought that chased the initial thought?'

He started jackhammering his knee. Updown, updown, updown-updown.

I wondered if I had pushed him too far. I reached out and placed my hand lightly on his leg. 'Anthony? What was your thought?'

'That I am a waste of a human. That I need to die. That I am a psycho.'

The self-appraisals come quickly, on each other's heels. We are so adept and speedy when it comes to judging ourselves.

'Okay, good.'

He looked up at me, and there was a sharp, surprised relief in his eyes.

'And now … ' I pointed to the next column. 'Now tell me, what evidence is there to support these thoughts?' We were detectives now, gigantic magnifying glasses pressed up to our eager faces.

Now Anthony was confused or wary or disdainful or a combination of these things. He looked from my face to the paper, my scrawlings there. What record were we creating? Who would see?

'The evidence is that I thought it.' He was shouting at me. 'The *fuck*?'

The magnifying glass had been tossed aside; this was not a case worth pursuing.

He was right. It was ridiculous. The columns on the page were not the point. They were just where we met. The meeting was the point.

He had stopped jackhammering his knee; all of his energy focused in incredulity, in rage.

I paused for a moment. 'This is for us only, Anthony. It is our work. No one else's.'

I breathed again. We are creatures of imitation and habit. Yawns, laughter – these are catching. I wanted him to catch the intention and depth of my breath. 'I know it seems it might be evidence of something, but it's not. It's *just* a thought. Have you ever physically hurt anyone before?'

He bent over, put his head between his knees in crash position, then sat up, face flushed, brow furrowed. 'No, but. You can't tell me someone who sees these things does not have some serious fucking screws loose.' He began jackhammering his knee again.

'There is no "but,"' I said. 'So it's only the thought that supports the thought, right? It's like this teetering house of cards. It's only built on itself. Experience tells us you are not a monster.'

'I'm still fucked.'

But I thought maybe he looked a little less sure. Or maybe just a little more spent. That was it. I had succeeded in completely exhausting him. 'How do you feel?' I asked. 'Where do you feel this in your body?'

'My *body*?' He laughed. 'How do *you* feel?'

I swore he was giving me the therapist face. I spoke firmly, bringing all my flimsy conviction and earthbound training to bear. 'I feel that you would never hurt me. I feel that you are not your thoughts. I know this from the evidence.' I point to the chart in my lap.

'But,' he says again. 'People change.'

Not often or easily, I want to tell him. And not in your case, right now. Oh, you are good. You are just a boy. You have had some bad things happen to you. You are sensitive and sad. You must switch the lens through which you see the world. But all this is easy for me to say. I am not where he is now. I see the terror there and the strain. What our minds are capable of. The scrims and obstacles they create. The paths we forge and deepen with our own skewed notions.

Love and listening cannot heal us; I understand that now. *The man's hand climbing up my rib cage; the music thumping within.* But perhaps a lack of judgment, of immediate diagnosis and rash prescription. A reticence to rush to solutions? A shared quiet? I want to, I need to, believe there is something in what I do.

ANTHONY

Go to the Paper Place, Ant.

Sam is sitting beside me. Sam is fiddling with her lip piercing. Sam is wearing a torn tank top and rubber bracelets. Sam has a row of tiny zits at her hairline. Sam's voice is weirdly husky when she is happy. Sam is a terrible skateboarder, but she tries her nuts off every time I dare her. Sam is so smart when it comes to art and such an idiot when it comes to life. Sam is ...

Sam? Someone needs to pay for what has happened to you.

What *is* happening to you?

Sam purses her lips, inhales an imaginary joint, then squints at me through the smoke. *Leave those poor suckers alone. Let them stew in their early adult, early twenty-first-century angst for a while longer. They do not concern you.*

I nod. Okay. Okay, Sam, okay.

Swear. Do I need to make you swear on my sword?

I shake my head no, then use the door frame to hoist myself upright.

If they are not to blame – and they are to blame, a little, a lot, in some way – then who is to blame?

Maria. I need to see Maria.

Ohmigawd, Anthony. Paper Place, you loser.

There is no hiding things from Sam. There has never been a way to hide things from her. But I need to see Maria.

The idea in the sessions with her was to find the cause, the deep root of these thoughts, which, she reassured me, were not my own. Which is a fine fucking thing to say, but what about the fact that they originate from my own fucking brain, you cunt? And who gives a rat's ass whose thoughts they are if they just won't stop coming? The Buddhists say thoughts are like clouds passing through your consciousness. Acknowledge them and leave them be. Go on your Buddhisty way. Except what if the clouds start raining blood? What if you wake up at 3 a.m. and the thought has arrived and set up camp in your brain and you think, *Of course this is what I want, this is my real self talking and I am a terrible, horrible, morally bankrupt mess?* Then what, youth counsellor? Take two free jelly beans and a complimentary condom and call you in the morning?

Oh, and just so you know, I stab myself too, in the thoughts. I'm an equal opportunity stabber.

Sam sighs. *Medal, Ant. You get the medal.*

Mostly school is better than home. Home is where the knives are. But even school is full of people with big cakeholes conversing and shit. Saying stuff to me or at me that could lead me to the thoughts or lead the thoughts straight to me. Maria called them 'intrusive thoughts'. Funny. Intrusive is like your neighbour popping his head over the fence during a family barbecue. Intrusive is a bad colour scheme in an otherwise tastefully decorated dining room. Intrusive is catching your parents in a horny embrace. Intrusive is hardcore interruption. But these thoughts are armed home invaders. Invasive. They are not messing around.

The kids in this classroom are crouched under the windows, huddled around the desks. They are maybe scared, maybe bored, probably annoyed. So be it. I try to remember which teacher might be in there with them. I think maybe Mr. Smith.

That's really his name. I'm probably the most white-bread kid in our whole multi-fucking-culti school, but even I am pretty sure a name like that doesn't really exist except in old-fashioned first-grade readers and in the text of math word problems. Mr. Smith should be wearing a suit and tie, a fifties-style fedora, carrying a briefcase full of important papers for other important middle-aged white men to sign. Instead, he dons Hawaiian shirts and these strange scarves whose ends hang down into the V of his sparse chest hair. What are those scarves even for? Sam said they're there because he teaches drama. She said he isn't gay but he isn't exactly straight either. I didn't ask her how she knew or what that meant he might do or be. I just believed her. Anyway, I don't think it's Mr. Smith in room 108. Maybe it's the pregnant one? She's nice; she smiled at me once when I came to drop off a late essay at the English office for Mr. Khan, who still wants us to print things even though, hello, there's this miracle called the internet. Sam had another pregnant one, Ms. Fellows, last year, and said it was hard to concentrate when she spoke because she grunted a lot. And it was like she couldn't hear herself doing it. That's a pregnant thing, I guess, Sam said. Thank Christ I'm never having kids. Me neither, I am thinking now. I would hurt them. They would just be staring at me all innocently, like, Okay, Dad, what next? Teach me to tie my shoe? Or read me a story? Catch a ball? And I'd be all like, Okay, right after I exorcise these bloody-minded demons from my brain pan. I don't know why I go a bit nineteenth-century as a dad but I do.

Or I'd be like my own dad. Hugging at all the wrong times and leaving trip hazards all around the house and thinking that if he stores his pot stash in a big white Tupperwaresque container labelled *Yitz's Gefilte Fish* no one will really know what's in there. Plus, we're not even Jewish.

I can imagine Sam's face all up in mine, the brown eyes wide with admiration and her particular brand of contempt.

Holy fucking shit, Ant, you got them to call a lockdown. You are some kind of high-level genius.

I'm on the genius spectrum, I tell her.

Fuck yeah, she says. *The spectrum. You need to move. They're gonna send in the po-po soon. Go to the Paper Place. You have the key, right?*

Yeah, yeah. I nod and pull it out of my pocket.

She throws back her head and laughs. *The key to the sanctuary for the man on the spectrum. Get up, Ant. Go.*

We have another place, our tree, down by the ravine. Sam carved our names into the trunk. SAM on one side and ANT on the other. No plus sign between us because it was never like that. Sometimes

I'd sit under her name and she'd sit under mine. That was how it was with us. Not like we added up to something, more like we could zoom in and out of each other's beings. Which sounds so fucking lame and sci-fi.

She hisses in my ear. *Paper Place.*

Ow. Okay, okay, I'm going. I push myself up the door the same way I got down and resist the urge to peer inside the small window at the top. It will be covered anyway, so the shooter has less visual access. 'Sorry,' I mouth to them. Poor suckers all trapped in there.

MARIA

She can already imagine the headlines, the clickbait they will make of this. It will become about the decline in family values, or the near-miss of the weaponry. Imagine if he'd had a gun! There will be some earnest think pieces about how, yeah, sure, we've done the kids wrong. But mostly they will remain our canaries in the coal mines, and when they respond as humans wounded by the poison in their surrounds, we will pathologize this too, blame the parents, the devices, the gays, the vaccinations, and not our massive lack of care for each other, for the earth ...

In the immediate aftermath – of what, exactly? She does not go there; she will not go there – a whole flotilla of grief counsellors will come sailing in on waves of solicitude. In the name of community, of healing, they will set up camp in tucked-away corners or over-exposed hallways, then be shocked when no students make use of their generously proffered services. For weeks, the school and its surrounds will enjoy or endure an increased police presence, then some professional development (an afternoon maybe?) on the precarity of youth mental health, where teachers will listen half-heartedly, or with a zeal that belies their deep fatigue. There will be walkie-talkies issued, new protocols around violence prevention developed and implemented. Zero tolerance, everybody will say, for bullying, for microaggressions, for inappropriate language, of course for knives, for guns, for fists and fury. And then? The counsellors will decamp, the police will disappear, the reporters will sniff out another hot spot, their gazes trained then flitting, distracted by what glints and bleeds and gives good crocodile tears, colourful images of strife and heartache. And maybe? In six months, or a year? A half-hearted follow-up piece, in which the perpetrator and victims are gamely humanized, the community interviewed for retrospective analyses, the school photographed in overcast morning light.

Why has he come back? Why did he have to come back?

There had been an odd calm to him that morning when he opened the door to her office. He had neatened his Whitney Houston concert tee (ironic?) with a quick, efficient tug before he stepped across the threshold. He trembled a little when she reached out to touch his shoulder.

'What happened?'

'Samantha,' he said. 'She is … lost.'

She nodded. Was Samantha gone and he could not bring himself to say it? Or was she actually lost, run away, misplaced? It seemed she had already been misplaced, by the universe, by this motherfucking institution, and she didn't strike Maria as a runner, more of a quiet resister … So, she was gone? The shock of this loss, this lostness, this howisshemissing, whathasshedone, sat on Anthony like the cloak of a royal. It gave him an odd solemnity; his anger had seemed teenaged, but his sorrow seemed elderly. For a moment, she was in awe of him. She was in awe of them all, these humans on the cusp, how wise and raw they were, how beautifully vulnerable.

'Do you want to talk about it?'

He began weeping then and she wanted to hold him; could she hold him? He must have seen her distress, how she was constrained still by her role, the thin veneer of professionalism, of distance and containment. He shook his head and reached for the Kleenex box, pulling a clump free, then holding the messy cloud up to his face. Then he spoke in a jumble, in a way both considered and nonsensical. He told her about Sam, his heart's sister, lying there lifeless or almost-so – Was that a breath? How he had held his phone to her lips like a mirror to see if she fogged it, and then – was that a smudge, condensation, or fingerprints? How he knew he had to call and then he did, but how would he explain how he knew how to climb the fire escape to her family's apartment, that she had copied him a key, that they had promised that nothing would ever be locked from the other? And when he got home, he knew he needed something to defend himself because Sam could not defend herself, but maybe he could protect them both, maybe it was his job to protect them both?

'Where is it, Anthony, where is the knife now?'

He had shrugged the bag from his shoulders. Army surplus, missing a buckle. He gestured to the main compartment.

And she had known what it meant. You could not bring a knife to school, no matter the threat to your own person. Because it compounded it, didn't it? Having a knife, a gun, was outside evidence of the impossibility of safety. And in this case, of course, of great grief and loneliness. She would have to report it.

'I'm so sorry, Anthony. You must go home. You have to go home.'

He nodded, then paused, then nodded again. Then he smiled in a way she found chilling not because of the potential violence it contained but because of its barely concealed disappointment in her and in the shaky edifice they had been building together.

He was right. She was doing more and less than she should. She should have picked up the phone with the expediency of a person trained in these protocols. Or she should have picked him up and smuggled him out of the building herself.

Instead, 'Please,' she said softly. And he had gone.

She sent a quick email to the VP: neutral, uninflected language.

And now? He was back. And some eye had caught him – camera or human. Back with a plan? Did he have a plan?

BLOOD

ELISE

The sound from the hallway has frozen us all in our slouching, semi-prone positions. What will happen next? Time billows, becomes bulbous with this question. Someone is there. In the first instant – how long does it last? – no one moves a muscle. It is cliché, but it is true, as if our bodies, like the bodies of animals – which they are – know to remain in place, breaths held, everything contracted, contracted. Still. Which is when I feel my belly go rock-hard, a band of pain around my lower back. I think I am the only one who notices, but when I look over at Shai-Anna, I know that she has seen it; her eyes are trained on my front-loaded bulk. Her gaze travels up and meets my own. She has seen and she knows.

'Don't worry,' I mouth as the pain subsides.

She looks back at me like I am the silliest white woman she has ever witnessed.

She is calling my bluff, but I won't let her in the midst of this … whatever we have found ourselves in. Some of the students have begun moving now, but slightly, pressing themselves up against the walls or slithering down so they are lying flat. Many of them have closed their eyes, as though thinking, in the way young children do, that if they cannot *see,* they cannot *be seen.*

There is a scuffling from outside. I hear some sharp intakes of breath and feel a gush between my legs. I hold my breath and wait for more noise from outside the room or more liquid from my body. But neither comes. So it is not my water breaking. But now there is a new noise and the person on the outside is trying the door, jiggling at the doorknob. Jennifer lets out a mouse-like shriek. Shilpa clamps a hand over Jennifer's mouth. Tears fall onto Shilpa's hand. I watch Jennifer's wide eyes fill and spill over. Then, footsteps. They are retreating, moving toward the main office and away from the classroom.

Time's membrane reforms around us.

We exhale.

Shilpa peels her hand carefully from Jennifer's mouth and Jennifer collapses into her friend's arms, where she begins sobbing softly. Loving murmurs are exchanged, hugs and gentle fist bumps. I take the opportunity to bend my head down between my knees, lifting up my dress so I can inspect the crotch of my grey leggings. There is a patchy circle of rusty red there. It is the Bloody Show. I know this with a cold certainty; there is no time for histrionics or my usual second, third, fourth guessings. The baby is not in danger, but the baby is coming. This is the Bloody Show. It is antiquated, Shakespearean-sounding. I am in blood stepped in so far … *steeped* in so far? I make a decision: the students don't need to know. Surely we will be released soon?

While I am conducting my crotch inspection, Shai-Anna has made her way over to my side. She is still sitting on the textbook, and the height gives her an erect, regal bearing next to my turtled form. She leans close.

'You're having contractions, aren't you?'

So much for restraint, for confidentiality, for professionalism and dignity. I meet her eyes and incline my head forward in what I hope is a subtle nod.

'Fuck.'

I nod again.

'We need to time them.'

'I've only had one,' I whisper. 'Could be a false alarm.'

'Miss,' she says, and rolls her eyes.

'Okay,' I say, 'but what makes you such an expert? Not parenting class.' The situation and my extreme expectant state have stripped me of tact and a certain politic falseness.

She smiles. 'Nah, my auntie had three babies and I was there to help with every single one.'

'Ah,' I say. I look around. 'We'll be out of here soon.' It's been fifty-three minutes. Typical, even for a drill, for them to take this long to check protocol. And, if something is truly wrong (something is wrong), they will have to strategize. They will be working hard – I propose to the panic merchants in my head – at keeping everybody safe.

'Still,' she says. 'You should time them.'

I nod again. But the action of timing still feels presumptuous, premature. But then it comes again. Not as strong this time but not small enough to hide from Shai-Anna, who gives me a pointed *You see what I mean, girl* look.

'Ryan,' I hiss out as the tightness fades. 'He needs something to do. To feel purposeful, y'know?'

Shai-Anna nods, then looks puzzled. 'Which one is he?'

'Vietnamese. In the corner.' I point as subtly as possible.

'On it,' Shai-Anna says, and begins a slow bum slide over to where Ryan is sitting, forehead to knees.

SHAI-ANNA

The kid Ryan looks up at me when I get close. Alarmed. I slide off the textbook into a crouch. It's stupid but I'm not ready to let my ass touch the floor yet.

'Hi?' says Ryan. Still scared.

And I guess he should be. Not of me but of whatever reason they have for locking us down. Of Miss Foster and her mega-pregnant body. 'Do you have a watch?' I know he does.

'Yes?' He holds up his wrist.

Two kids sitting against the radiator start laughing. At Ryan? I cut my eyes at them and they sort of stop, but then start up again.

'Why?' says Ryan, still holding up his wrist.

I want him to stop addressing me with one-word questions and freaked-out eyebrows.

'We need you to time contractions.' I bounce a little in my crouch and jerk my head toward Miss.

'Contractions?' The wrist comes down.

'Yes, contractions.' I watch this register. The eyebrows settle into a frown.

'Okay,' Ryan says. 'Yes, I can do that.' He taps the face of the watch and it bleeps like it knows something.

I allow myself to feel a tiny bit of respect for him. We do a kind of fucked-up army crawl back to the corner. I mostly keep my eyes on Miss as we go but I can feel the rest of them and their cunty curiosity coming at me. It's low-key irritating. I don't need them to be my friends but holy fuck. There is a possibility unreeling in my head. That this will be where it happens, that a baby will be born.

'Hi, Ryan,' says Miss. 'Glad you could make it.' She laughs.

Adults are weird.

Ryan has taken up his post. He pinches the watch; it bleeps twice. His eyes meet mine.

ELISE

'What's going on?' Faduma mouths at me insistently, a small terror tugging at the corners of her lips.

I know there can be no hiding now. I point at my belly and shrug again, smiling.

'No,' she mouths.

''Fraid so,' I whisper back. 'We need to get things ready.'

She crawls over to me. 'We need … Miss, what do we need?'

I can see that while I am still able, it will be my job to delegate, to assign tasks, to make these young people feel powerful in what has become a situation that makes them feel powerless in triplicate. I scan the classroom. 'Blankets. Or as close to. Water.'

'Okay,' says Faduma. 'I can do this.'

I watch her eyes skimming the people in the room, checking to see what items of clothing can be easily, modestly, shed. Rahid and Tiffany and Bianca are huddled together, protecting whatever is playing on one small screen.

'I need your hoodies,' she says to Rahid and Tiffany. 'And your scarf.' To Bianca. 'Miss is maybe going to have her baby.'

They look mildly shocked, then shrug themselves out of their clothes quickly, hand them over.

Next I watch her pluck a small pad of fluorescent Post-it notes from the folds of her dress. She sticks four together, then writes in block letters across them: WHO HAS A WATER BOTTLE? Then she sticks the whole message to the front of her hijab so it hangs down like a shutter to her eyebrows.

FADUMA

I begin in the corner with the two girls huddled together next to Thanh, who is still sleeping, a little bubble of spit just hanging at the corner of his lips, which are pink and full, I notice, then quickly unnotice because lips make me think of kissing and that is *haram*. The girls, whose names are Tania and Charlotte (or Charlene?), look up at me quickly, their eyes skimming over my Post-it message. They frown in unison, then Charlene/Charlotte goes digging in her backpack and pulls out one of those pricey designer stainless-steel bottles with a pastel cloud design on it. She shakes it.

'Not much left,' she says, and shrugs but passes it over.

Tania just twists her mouth at me and reaches for her phone. Next are Isaiah and Kevin and Julie.

'Is she, like, dehydrated?' Kevin sounds alarmed, so I try to sound knowledgeable.

'No, we just need a lot of water for the process, you know?' I am acting all professional like I've done this before, but it's hard because of the Post-its, which I now realize are less clever than ridiculous. Because obviously I am talking to people. But Kevin looks like he's bought it. He hands over his plastic water bottle, which is totally full.

'How close is she to, like, giving birth?' Julie says. 'Is she really having her baby here? I'm pretty sure we should call 9-1-1. Like, a second 9-1-1. Imagine if she dies or the baby dies. My mom's friend's baby died because the cord strangled it.' She lifts her hands and grips her neck to demonstrate, going all bug-eyed and red.

'She says she's okay. That we'll be out of here soon.'

Julie frowns. 'I mean, I guess. Pregnant lady's wishes.'

Isaiah has turned away from the conversation and is looking kind of frantically in his bag for something. Not a bottle – his earbuds and a pack of gum, which he slides open, snapping two squares from their foil pods and passing them to Julie and Kevin.

'Water?' I'm pissed off now but trying not to show it because, stupidly, I still want these people to like me.

'Oh no, sorry no. I just use the fountain, the one near the office that's not nasty.'

'Whatever,' I say, but he doesn't hear. He's chewing his gum and the earbuds are nestled in.

Next are Fatou, Emily, and Renata.

'Ohmigod, is she okay?' says Emily. 'Can I help? How can I help?' I've known her since middle school. Super-fake and irritating and I don't trust her. Kids used to call her Cat-shit Slutivan, for a reason nobody remembered. Which was mean.

'We got this. But do you have any water?' I'm in charge here.

Fatou reaches behind her and pulls out a school water bottle. 'It's got mint tea in it,' she says.

'Is that healthy for pregnant women?' says Emily. 'I read there are some things that are, like, toxic.'

'I was saving it for later,' says Fatou. 'But I guess she needs it more?'

Renata just stares at me, then begins nodding and doesn't stop. Who is the nodding even for? I heard she gave Mark a blow job under the stairs near the science lab once. Not even in a bathroom stall or anything. And I can believe it but I know I shouldn't because there is actually such a thing as fake news. Anyway, it is not for me to judge. That's Allah's job. Even though sometimes I want so badly to judge. Next is a group of boys playing poker. They don't really notice me, but two of them pass over their bottles and one of them – I think his name is Gaurav – points at my Post-its and laughs in a kind of approving way. I pull the message down, scrunch the paper up, and scan the room. Six more people until I reach Mark. But who's counting? I am. I am counting so hard.

I've had dreams about him. He does this thing in my dream where he runs his fingers gently down the side of my cheek, then holds the edge of my hijab between his pointer and thumb like it is a precious thing he respects but he would still like to lift it gently from my head. Then he bends down and kind of nudges at my face with his chin so I have to look up, and when I look up he kisses me. And his lips are so soft and I get these explosions in my belly and this feeling of happiness so intense it's like being electrocuted. And then I wake up. So you can see how conversation is going to require some of what my AP psych teacher would call compartmentalizing. And even though, like I said, organization is my thing, I haven't quite mastered how to put that feeling in a box in my head so the contents don't leak out all over my face and stop me from forming coherent sentences when he is around.

'I think there's actually a regulation against this,' says Alison, who is up next. 'She can't actually have her baby here. There's health and safety stuff. And also, it's just a bit negligent, right, amirite? I mean, her primary responsibility is to us, but she can just go ahead and have a baby in the middle of class time? Who is supervising us now? So lame.' She tries to catch some eyes for validation, but no one is biting.

'Can I have your water bottle?' I hold out my hand.

'Whatever.' She passes it over to me.

And now it's Mark.

'Hey,' I say. 'Got any water or water bottles?' My voice goes a bit lost on that last part, like I'm not sure I mean what I'm saying. NOT profesh.

Still, he nods and passes me this old-school thermos thing. 'How is she? Is she for real giving birth?'

'I think so,' I say.

'Shit,' he says. 'That's what's up.'

'Facts,' I say. 'But hopefully we'll be out of here soon.'

'K, well let me know if you want me to do anything. I mean, maybe not anything with the actual you know, but … '

'Thanks,' I say. 'I gotta get these back.' I jerk my chin toward the pile of bottles.

'Here,' he says. 'Take my bag.' He upends it and a few crumpled sheets of lined paper and a gym shirt fall out.

He helps me put the water bottles into his bag, and Allah forgive me, I can smell him and it is like the smell of something holy and unholy at once.

ELISE

Shai-Anna has returned with Ryan in tow. And sure enough, his watch is well-suited. It has many functions and buttons only he knows how to operate.

'Good call, Miss,' says Shai-Anna grudgingly. 'He knows what to do. Just tell him when one starts and when it ends.'

Ryan crouches awkwardly at my feet. 'Come sit up here,' I tell him. I point to the space next to my belly. He presses his watch buttons and they beep in response.

Then he waddles up, rocks back onto his bum. 'Are you ... are you in pain, Miss?'

'Nah, not yet. But I will be. I need you to not mind too much about that, okay? I need you only and always to do your job. Can you do that? Can you do that for me, Ryan?'

'Yes.' He caresses the face of his watch.

'Okay, good. You know how I am with time.' It's true, I am forever being interrupted mid-thought by the bell, entreating them all to stay put while I hurriedly assign reading or offer reminders.

There is another noise from the hallway, a new shuffling loudness. We pause again in our actions, as if the needle has been lifted from the record.

'Oh God,' I groan – quite loudly, I imagine – as another contraction overtakes me. I give Ryan a signal – how, I'm not sure – and he begins to time, pressing the button with authority. The contraction takes me, squeezes my self out. When I come back, there is a soft rhythmic sound coming from the region of the door.

'Is someone ... knocking?' I ask Faduma. My vision is hazy and I expect my hearing is also fuzzy; I do not trust my senses to report back accurately from the outside world anymore. The sound comes again, more percussive and insistent this time.

'Yes,' says Shai-Anna. 'Some motherfucking asshole is knocking.'

And it comes to me, like the memory of a dream comes – in dragging threads and tendrils – that this is Samara knocking. 'Samara,' I say to Ryan, who looks down at his watch, places the pads of his fingers on the buttons. 'It's Samara.' I have turned to Shai-Anna now, who is sucking her teeth. 'You have to let her in.'

Faduma is the one who passes the word down the row of kids. It is novel to them, this message being handed along without the benefit of electronics; it is intimate. Heads lean softly into ears, lips approach with the breathy message. 'It's Samara. Let her in.'

When the message reaches Mark, who is closest to the door, I watch a transformation occur. He has been playing a video game, jaw clenched in concentration, but now the jaw slackens. He turns to confirm with the speaker, who nods and points up to the door. We know the risk we are taking, the risk we have transferred to his shoulders, broad and young (and innocent) as they may be. I can see the realization when it hits his eyes. He stands deliberately. A cat burglar or a marine. I want to laugh. I am so proud of him.

I taught him before – when he was a different boy, an earlier, angrier boy. In Grade 10 he would write me journal entries about his grandmother, whom he adored, but not much else. When he came to class, it was to skulk in the corner, hoodie pulled forward like a monk. His was the kind of anger that surrounded him like a fog. It was hard to see him through the scrim, and he squinted up at me as if I were unreal or an intrusion. Which I suppose I was. Once, when I got exasperated because he would not put away his phone or meet my eye, he stood up and upended his desk. The movement was fluid and frightening. He stalked out of the room and I let him. When the hall monitor asked what had happened, I was at a loss. History happened, I wanted to say.

The one time Mark did not write about his grandmother, he wrote about his skin. I pinned the three scrawled sentences to my bulletin board. *Being Black is like a job I do every single fucking day. When I wake up and go out the door when I get on the bus when I hang out with my friends when I go to the corner store when I come to school I'm doing my job. When I don't do my job properly I get punished and most of the time I have no fucking clue how to do my job.*

Mark lifts the corner of the chart paper to peer out – a quick pick at the masking tape with his fingernail and up it comes, a little flap flipped up to show us the world, just as quickly pressed down again.

He turns toward us, his audience. 'It's Samara,' he confirms. A racket of birdsong erupts from the courtyard. Another world exists! But it is not our world.

Mark meets my eye.

'Open it,' I say. 'Let her in.' He breathes in shallowly, a breath that does not reach his diaphragm but balloons his pecs impressively. Then he reaches for the door handle, turns it, reaches out, and pulls Samara inside.

Samara falls at his feet, a pile of faded blue jeans, fuchsia glasses, hijabbed bun, and Peter Pan boots. Also, many rolls of toilet paper and a pile of brown institutional paper towel. She pushes herself up and scans the room until she finds me.

'Hey, Miss. It's been a minute.'

I nod.

'Is it true?'

I raise my eyebrows. Why is she making this into a coffee-shop conversation?

'Is it true you're having your baby?'

I nod again. The other students – even the ones who know – turn to me with WTF all over their faces.

'Sorry,' I say. 'I can't control it. How did you know?'

Samara shrugs. 'Shai-Anna texted me. That's why I brought these.' She prods at the toilet rolls with her foot. 'I heard him. The intruder, I mean. He passed by the bathroom. I think … maybe someone was with him?' The anxious uplift at the end of her sentence, the catch in her voice.

She is feigning nonchalance. God, what it must cost them! To know it all when you have lived so little. It is possible I will have my baby here. Some brash teenager will catch her in a scratchy-ass paper towel. And Jesus, I want my husband so badly I can feel it in my cunt. I can't help it; I begin to cry.

Faduma notices first. A Siberian friend once explained to me the notion of 'skinless people' in her aboriginal culture. I suspect Faduma is one of these people, vulnerable to the world in a way that is both wondrous and dangerous.

'It's okay, Miss. We'll take care of you. And we'll probably get out of here soon, get you to a hospital. I mean … it takes a long time to have a baby.'

It is both discomfiting and oddly cheering to feel the reversal that has occurred, to witness her attempts at reassuring me.

'You have another child, though, right, Miss? This your second?' Shai-Anna asks.

'Yes,' I say, surprised at my meekness in offering up this information. 'I have a seven-year-old. Joey.'

'So your body knows what to do. Could be quick.' Shai-Anna appraises me reproachfully.

I shrug. I'll take it. The comfort. The reproach. I don't have much choice.

Faduma is frowning at her phone. 'My dad is texting,' she says. 'What do I tell him?'

'Tell him we are all safe,' I say, suddenly again-authoritative. 'Tell him we will let him know when the lockdown is lifted. Tell him he should check the school website. Call the number specifically designated for this situation.' The words feel hollow and bullshitty even to my own ears.

'What about … ?' says Faduma, and points to my belly.

'God, no! I mean, just tell him you are fine.' I am surprised at my own adamancy. Is it denial? An ill-timed bid for privacy? A preference for the devil I know? Maybe. Or I want to protect those on the outside from what is happening – what the fuck *is* happening? – here.

Someone has pinned up a comic over the photocopier in the staff room. Two people with large blocky bodies and rectangular heads leaning toward each other in a booth at a diner, sharing confidences. 'I went into teaching because I've always loved crazy parents,' says one to the other.

Ha! The parents *are* crazy. Some of them more than others, granted. What a strange thing, to suddenly find myself among them. To realize there are things I would do for my own children, unthinkable things.

Bizarre, isn't it, how every experience we have, no matter how small and inconsequential, invites us into a society of others, a new slew of humanity? Aha, here you are, welcome to the club. Oh, your dad had a heart attack? My dad had a heart attack! And me too! I also got drunk on peach schnapps when I was fourteen! Yes, they follow me in the dollar store too. Next time go with a white friend. Different story, fam. I experience a transcendent joy when I am anywhere near a birch tree. You too? Ass slapped? Tit pinched? Check, check. And now? My kid had pinworms too! Greetings, comrade. You know it comes from eating poo, right? So gross. Hello, friend.

It is perhaps old-fashioned to believe that we are all part of a whole. Much more seemly these days for us to stay standing in our silos, unknowable. But there it is: I got into teaching for the crazy parents. I *am* a crazy parent.

I remember the first time I understood Joey to be completely separate from me – a universe unto himself. He was almost three, still in his cot. I had stroked his back, sung my catalogue of songs with great feeling (only occasionally feigned), and in my mind I was already out the door, down the stairs, checking email, switching the laundry over.

'Mama,' he said, after I'd bid him good night. 'Do that smile for me. The bedtime smile.'

My god, I thought, the kid knows my repertoire of smiles. To be known, to be observed like that – it is deeply flattering and unnerving. I mustered my best 'gazing down at child' smile and I passed the test somehow. I passed. Still, I know there will come a day when the answers I offer will feel ragged, incomplete, or, worse still, like outright lies. I think of this and the inevitable ways we let down our children when I reread Mark's words or when I wash up on the shores of 3 a.m. some restless nights.

It is in these moments I question this whole project I have embarked upon – this business of growing and birthing new humans.

What in heaven's name was I thinking?

I was thinking of animal smells and skin-to-skin closeness, balls thrown, fumbled, caught, bedtime stories in perpetuity … I was not thinking about social media's strange byways, hormonal surges, and slammed doors. Of droughts, fires, pandemics, an atmosphere rife with curses and carcinogens. It terrifies me – the road I see stretching out before me, and the inextricability of these bonds I am forging. This job I can never, ever quit.

I feel another contraction coming and elbow Ryan, harder than is warranted, in the ribs.

All of my fortune-telling and forensic philosophizing evaporates while I am in the contraction's clutch. I fixate on a group of students huddled over by the radiator. Are they cold? No, they are pointing at me, making large gestures.

When the contraction finally subsides, I understand what is happening. They are making a plan.

ENG4U1-03

Someone starts a group chat. So we can make a *plan*. The plan centres on creating a flexible human shield to smuggle Miss out of the building. It is not a very honed plan and there seem to be shifting parameters; its leaders are various and constantly changing in the group chat that has been created to contain and further the plan. There are discussions about exits and possible weapons and stealth manoeuvres. There are arguments about who is best suited for which role in the escape. There are memes to break up the relentlessness of the texts. The memes are ironic. The memes often involve possums or hedgehogs. We misunderstand each other and use caps to yell our rage and for emphasis because this is an EMERGENCY. We wonder what we will do if the baby gets stuck because that is something that happens, we have heard. We wonder what our parents are thinking, or we share their panicked texts and the NBD ways we have responded. We wonder: Is it true, has the intruder taken a *hostage*? We try to stay on track, on message, on brand. This is a planning thread. How can we smuggle Miss past the shooter to safety? We are not thinking about ourselves or our mortality or our need for love and acceptance and all the things we have yet to experience and accomplish. *Methinks the lady doth protest too much.* One of us complains that this is all Miss's fault anyway. And another says no, it's just fate, it's no one's fault. And another one says, yeah, but who controls our fate, dumbass? And someone else says God. And someone else says I don't think so. And someone else says I'm a Gemini so fate is kind of neither here nor there for me. And someone else says are you guys hungry? And someone else says it's only been one hour forty-five minutes and someone else says actually one hour forty-seven minutes and someone else says can we get back to the plan and someone else says we can't let him in and someone else says we've got to get her out and then a possum holding a machine gun

ELISE

I can feel Faduma's hands now at the base of my neck; she is squeezing experimentally, tentatively, so I lean into her, consenting, and she massages at the tight muscles there, first gently, and then more firmly, with a healer's intuition. The number of boundaries we are crossing here is astounding, but I trust her, as I hope she trusts me. She has a lot of rules for herself, I can tell, but also an expansiveness of spirit that emerges in quick flashes in her journal responses or in the sweet absorption of her bowed form during independent reading.

It's true that we complain about a lot of things in my profession. It's why outsiders hate us, but it's mostly for protection, a kind of in-the-trenches deflection. We all have our secret joys when it comes to the job. Mine, especially since I became a parent myself, is the parent-teacher interview. I understand how urgent and mysterious and important it feels to speak to the person who witnesses your child when they are out of your orbit – what an intense pleasure to hear they are engaged and sociable and excelling, and what a heart-rending event to learn they have been skipping class, smelling of weed, or coming to class regularly, assiduously turning in assignments but refusing to speak, moping in the corner. Mostly, I enjoy it so much, being this fortune teller – except when parents size me up with skepticism, examine the subversive student work on the walls with something approaching dread, question my records or means. It is their prerogative of course and perhaps only natural I would feel defensive and have to manage my defensiveness with polite smiles and a forced, open posture.

It is important to learn as much as I can about a student in these meetings – their circumstances and context. There are times the interviews unlock a secret that has been lurking in the slouch and shout of a teen – oh, they help at their father's corner store till all hours! Oh man, their mother is in cancer treatment ... Fuck, this uncle/guardian is so creepy and controlling! At other times, the parents come to me already stricken and helpless, their palms upturned in surrender. We don't know what else to do, they say with their eyes or their mouths, and I have no choice but to offer platitudes and weak suppositions. I don't know, I want to say, how much harder you can love this child. I don't know why she has gone off the rails, down the wrong path with the wrong crowd and oh, I see your fatigue and emptiness, I do.

Faduma's father came to the last parent-teacher conference, a tall imposing man in a salwaar kameez and intricate kofia. I rose to my feet as he entered – as a sign of respect. And to make myself taller. Then I extended my hand.

'Hello,' I said. 'You must be Faduma's dad.'

'Yes,' he said. 'Good evening.' He looked pointedly at the hand I had proffered, then looked away. 'I cannot shake your hand,' he said. 'Surely you know this?'

'Oh,' I said, flustered. 'I'm sorry. Please sit.'

He lowered himself into the orange plastic chair fussily, brushing at the seat on the descent.

I became suddenly aware of the way my breasts were spilling out of the top of my blouse, my belly straining against the buttons. I was not wearing a wedding ring, never have. The tea that was rapidly cooling on the desk in front of me was housed in a cracked mug someone had left in the English office cupboard. It had a vodka company logo emblazoned on the side.

Unmarried.

Alcohol-swilling.

Fecund and fleshy.

Amazing how instantaneously, how completely, one can judge oneself through another's eyes.

I opened my marks-record binder and found Faduma's name. 'I have no real concerns about Faduma, Mr. Hassan. She is a hard-working student and bright. Always asking good questions.'

Mr. Hassan looked down at the binder spread-eagled between us. 'And her mark?'

'Well,' I said, 'it looks like she's at a seventy-eight.'

'Ah,' he said. 'Why?'

I cleared my throat. 'She's done well on the reading and speaking/listening assessments, but writing is ... inconsistent. I think her perfectionism keeps her from handing things in on time, or at all. Oh, and here is a media mark that is low.'

'Media?' he said, and seemed to scoff. Then he stood, effectively bringing our meeting to a close. 'I will talk to her. She must turn her work in.'

I sighed and cradled my belly. I had snitched on Faduma. 'Thank you,' I said, 'for coming.'

I did not give his retreating back the finger because I am too much my mother's daughter. Instead, I pulled my blouse together and attempted to fasten another button. I walked over to the chalkboard and erased a small rocket-shaped penis someone had scrawled in the corner underneath my homework reminders.

FADUMA

I wonder if it might be possible to be friends with Shai-Anna. Weirdly, she reminds me a little of my dad, which is both a pro and a con. I try to picture sitting next to her in the stairwell, laughing at some lame thing one of us said that has, through some miracle, crossed over into comedy genius. I have not laughed, not fully, for a long time. The last time I remember really losing it was when Rukiya inhaled a strand of spaghetti through her nose and somehow made it come out through her mouth. She said she learned it from her uncle, who did weird tricks like that when everyone was chilling at the house after performing salat at the masjid. I even peed my pants a little, and when I told everybody I was peeing, that made us all laugh harder so we couldn't even talk or breathe. We were all just gasps and hiccups. I've never laughed like that with my non-Muslim friends. Which doesn't mean that I couldn't. Or that I shouldn't. It just means that I can't really see it happening. And I'm not even sure I want it to happen.

Shai-Anna is conscripting people, telling them what to do in no uncertain terms. They don't look happy, but they don't look pissed off either. Mostly she is just asking them not to be dumbasses about the fact that their teacher keeps doing squats and making really freaky sounds. She has decreed a law about social media sharing.

'Sharing is not fucking caring when it comes to letting the outside world, including the intruder, know that we have a vulnerable person in our midst.'

She actually said that. *In our midst.*

ANTHONY

It is not far down the hallway to the staff room and the paper room is nestled inside it like the hard little baby in a Russian doll, but still I find my body slowing, getting sluggish – the opposite of my stealth coming up the stairs. I don't want to leave the orbit of room 108. It's like they have something in there I can never have.

What the fuck, Ant? They're just boneheaded teenagers like us.

Innocence, my self whispers. They have innocence.

You are fucking kidding me. You haven't done anything except make the mistake of narcing on yourself to an adult with too many regulations carved into their cerebellum.

'But I couldn't save you.' I say it out loud, all strangled and sad, then clamp my hands over my mouth like a cartoon character. Sam doesn't answer. I hope she didn't hear me. She doesn't go in for melodrama or retrospective moaning. I drag myself through the main foyer.

Fo-yuhr or fo-yay depending on your preference or provenance, says Sam in a singsongy British voice.

To my right is a display commemorating missing and murdered Indigenous women – mannequins in red dresses and a poster of a medicine wheel. I blink and see the mannequins as they are – foam torsos draped in fabric. Then I blink again. Headless women bathed in blood. Can I make you understand that when I see these things I know that I am responsible? Not that I *could* be responsible. Nuh-uh. Sense and time fold in on themselves. I *am* responsible. I feel the blood dripping onto my shoe.

Sam heaves another mega-sigh. *Ew. Ant. Paper Place.*

I walk into the staff room, past a bulletin board crowded with notices for union meetings and teacher discounts. The main lounge is empty and beige, nothing new. My dad told me that when he was in high school his social science teacher would duck out of the classroom to have a smoke and place bets on the horse races in the staff room. When he came back he'd be calmer and more chatty; he'd call the girls Darlin' and the boys Champ. Sometimes he'd give them the answers to the multiple-choice quizzes, mouthing the sequence of letters with a wink. Not many teachers hang out in the staff room these days. They stay in their offices with their phones and their microwaves. Unless it's to nap sitting up, slumped on the oversized couch cushions.

The Paper Place is behind the photocopier, which is still humming, buttons glowing blue. Like it didn't get the lockdown memo. I try the door. It doesn't give.

The keys.

Right, the keys. There are three of them on the ring. I wonder which doors the other two unlock. Bluebeard's castle; a room full of dead wives? Sam whispers the code stamped on the correct key into my ear. I find it and insert it into the lock. And just like that, I'm in.

This is the one place in the school I feel safe. The space is slightly bigger than a walk-in closet. Like a run-around-in closet. And I've thought about it, what it might be like to actually live in here. Not so bad, if someone brought me soft food and I had a few inoffensive books and my music. I don't actually get why jail is seen as punishment; it seems to me like it could be a kind of safe escape.

I walk over to the corner farthest from the door, behind a wall of filing cabinets. I can sort of crouch here and not be seen. Around me, on either side, are stacks and stacks of paper, wrapped tightly like presents, piled like bricks. I crouch in my spot and practise stillness. Which is something Maria would like. Me, being still, surrounded by all these white sheets of blankness. I think about paper cuts, and for once it does not send me to stabbing, to knives. Not true, it totally does, but I rein myself in and imagine instead all those sheets of paper coming at me, all those sharp edges slicing me, leaving tiny cuts all over my body. And I think about how comforting, how absolutely awesome, that would be.

We did this poem in English class last month when I was still making it to a few classes. It was really all about paying attention to nature and shit, but there was this one line that stuck with me: *Imagination is better than a sharp instrument.* And I thought, wow, did she ever get that wrong. Imagination *is* a sharp instrument, poet lady. Imagination is a knife made for stabbing.

I knew I could tell Sam about the thoughts because she's a Bengali-Canadian lesbian who cuts herself. Once they made us do these flower-of-power things in class. On each petal you put something that society judges you by – culture, gender, sexuality, class. Everybody thought that last one was like, how classy you were and you could tell they were all puzzled and shit because it sounded really British and James Bond. But it really means how much money your parents make. Which I knew but would never say out loud. Anyway, when we did that flower, I was sitting next to Sam and she showed me her petals and said, 'So, basically, I'm fucked.' Then she made this face that said even though my petals essentially predicted I would one day be master of the universe, she still saw the freak in me and very possibly understood how fucked I was too. And I think that's when we became friends, although I can't be sure because it seems to me that the really important people in your life – you can't trace them back to one seed or spark. It's like they've just always been there. Sam tells me all this nasty shit about stuff she'd like to do with women, which is why I thought maybe she wouldn't puke in my face if I told her what my brain kept uploading. But still, I waited for a good time.

We were in our place down by the creek, a couple blocks away from the school, sitting with our backs against the same tree trunk but looking out in different directions. We're good at talking this way. Sometimes we even hold hands, but lightly, sort of like we have paws instead of complicated fingered things. And she was telling me about Jacinta, this shorty she met online who was older and femme and really into feminist theory with great little tits and stony grey eyes.

'She's amazing,' Sam said.

And I got ready to listen to the catalogue of acts she would perform on this Jacinta, when I heard her take a long shuddery breath and I knew she was crying. I put my paw on top of hers.

'But I don't love her, Ant. I won't ever love her.'

'Why not,' I asked, but it was almost a whisper. I know exactly why people can't love because I know my own self. It's because there is a deep dark hurt thing they need to protect. I wanted Sam to let go of her thing, to let it out of its cage so I could see it; I'd help her look at it and then lock it up again or kill it even.

I wanted to tell her about what I saw last summer. My parents were having a party and I'd just come in from playing basketball outside when I heard a noise in the kitchen. I'm a pretty mediocre basketball player but it used to be that basketball was the only thing that helped me feel normal again. A couple years ago Sam was over at my house and she pulled a book from our bookshelf. It was poetry by John Ashbery. She started reading the poems out loud, dancing around while she did it. At one point she was bent over the kitchen island, twerking, while she recited his stuff. It was not rhymy or flowery at all – the poetry, not the twerking – it was more like sentences that had been written with thought dyslexia. Ideas that were hard to get a hold of. But there was one line that stayed with me. 'As steam from a wet shingle, and I am happy once again.' That line I understood completely. That was what they meant when they said, Oh, he's just letting off some steam. That it could be less about anger and more about this release, a cloud of the thing that blocked your happiness rising up into the air. Anyway, that's how I feel when I play basketball. The sound of the ball on the pavement, *thwuc, thwuc, thwuc*. The moment when the ball balances on the rim. And it doesn't really matter if the ball goes in or not, because both options offer possibilities. The possibility, that pause, is *everything*. I could live in that pause.

Anyway, I was in that zone when I heard the noise from inside, the noise that was almost not a noise. If I was like that poet lady I might say something lame like it was a resounding absence of noise. There were only a couple of people left in the house and one of them was passed out on the living room couch. I passed by her, my ma's friend Jacky, I could tell by the tightness of her jeans, the way some skin was chubbing out at the top. And her breathing too. I didn't want to think about what it meant that I could recognize my ma's BFF's passed-out breathing. I just wanted a drink of water and to lay me down to sleep.

When I walked into the kitchen, I saw my dad first. He was in a kind of animal crouch in the corner. His arms were up over his head like he was afraid the sky might fall on him. And there was my ma standing over him. I couldn't see his face, but I could see hers. She was wearing a mask, I thought. But then her eyebrows moved when she saw me, and I thought, Not a mask. A spell. It was like those before-and-after makeover shows and the Big Reveal, the big reveal was that my mother felt nothing. There was a knife in her hand. Go away, she said to me, but her lips didn't move. It was like she was the ventriloquist *and* the puppet. Get out. My dad made a sound like he was trying not to puke and then he pissed himself. I've had enough, said my mother. I threw my basketball at her, passed it hard into her gut. Then her face crumpled and she was sunk down, sobbing, on the floor next to him. Her face was blotchy and red next to my father's, and they were holding on to each other like they were the last two suckers left on some shit-ass life raft. I knew that Sam would understand the fucked-upedness of that night. And also that it was my family, and that meant something too.

But when I turned to look at her, she had a razor blade out and was drawing it slowly across the skin above her ankle. The blood beaded there, then joined up and snailed down into her sock.

Once in class Sam and I were partners for a poster on a literary device and we just turned every thought we had into a rhetorical question. We would text each other that way because it made everything feel less serious. Because the answers weren't important. They were just kind of floating in the atmosphere. Why do we have a little extra fleshy thing that hangs down at the back of our throats? Don't answer that. It was purely rhetorical. Who is in charge here? No real answer. Purely rhetorical. Are you high? Rhetorical, dude. What is the purpose of self-harm?

I used to think I was in love with Sam because I knew she would beat the shit out of anyone who ever tried to hurt me. We made out one night when we were both drunk and high, before I stopped drinking and smoking, scared of the sloppiness of it. Scared of what I might do. She didn't mention the kiss the next day so I didn't either. I thought maybe it was just that we kind of fell into each other and our lips did this thing. Now I think I wasn't in love with her at all. Maybe I just wanted to be her.

SAM

I know for sure that you will be okay, Ant, that this will not break you. You are made for this world in a way I am not, maybe never was. I know you can endure what is just momentary atmosphere for you, despite the fact that it keeps pinning you to a target and chucking knives your way. My certainty is an eggplant colour – deep, rich, dark, shiny, a not-quite blood that reflects light but won't give back an image. Super-goth, I know, Ant, but it's true, you know I don't do sweetness and light. I like it dirty, I like it doomsday. And I feel this certainty in the tips of my nipples, lightly, a tingling. I feel this certainty in my lower belly. I'd say my womb, but I'm not sure I have one. I'm all Lady Macbeth, getting demons to suckle, y'know? I end with me. I've tried to fight this by joining myself to other people, climbing into their bodies. Tongues clashing, fisting. Then again, then again. It will hurt you to hear this when my certainty is a gift to you, but I have been wrong before. I was wrong about you, Ant. I thought you looked like the biggest dick when we got paired for that exercise. I thought you looked like the Enemy. I knew, in fact, in my deepest cunt, that you were my opp and not worth my time or energy, not even the disdain required for a quick side-eye. And now look at us! Can you believe us? Don't answer that: purely rhetorical.

ELISE

Giving birth to my first child was probably the truest most uncluttered instance in my life. I fell clean away from what was expected or controlled, jumped off the tracks, out of the groove. The rules that used to apply wobbled or just imploded into incoherence. I had no words. I'm still not sure I have words. My utterances took the form of a more earthen language, full of dirt, blood, sorrow, and yearning. How can I do that here, with these children? I want to go home, to be with someone who might understand. And I think Nate would. Understand, that is.

I have never strayed from my marriage. The language sounds old-fashioned even to me. I don't find this fact praiseworthy or noble. In fact, there are times I berate myself. Such cowardice – to not have seized opportunities for fulfillment and expansiveness when they presented themselves. To be left instead with a great longing for what could have been, especially at times like these, when the universe presses itself down upon me.

It was in the early days of us, pre-kids, pre-mortgage, when we were still jaggedy with ourselves, finding a way forward as a couple, throwing objects in passion in our small galley kitchen, careful never to hit each other, but enjoying the force and show of our feeling. I went to a five-day conference in Stratford, Ontario – Bringing the Bard to the Youth. I had opted for a small inn over the larger chain hotel suggested and discounted in the conference package. It was brownstone, three storeys, with bathrooms in every room, but still a modicum of forced intimacy with other guests – meals served at set times in a dining room decked out in Victorian antiques. I was happy to sit by myself, hands wrapped gladly around my coffee cup, watching the finches that came to the feeder. I felt grown-up, disdainful and admiring of the doilies scattered on the tables, hyper-aware of my status as educator, as the epitome of anti-old maid/school marm. I was a little in love with my own self and high on that feeling. I wasn't looking for distraction or sex or any type of subversive liaison. I was happy. So when Devin sat down at the table next to mine, my first thought was that he was blocking my view of the feeder and my next that he looked pretentious, probably gay, and definitely defensive about both of these aspects of himself.

I was surprised when he half jumped out of his chair, making the place settings jive a little in place, then sat down quickly, pointing joyfully to the feeder.

'Rose-breasted finch! Not often you see those!'

The next day the owner of the inn gave us sunflower seeds and we stood in the back garden with our palms outstretched. The birds landed like thoughts, their pronged feet gentle and insistent. A feeling rose in me, from my womb to my throat. It was not like orgasm, nor was it like any other kind of joy or satisfaction I had ever experienced. Was it religious? I didn't want to try to describe it in case I diffused it. When I looked over at Devin, quickly, quickly, so as not to miss the rapid proddings and peckings of those tiny beaks in the flesh of my hand, I could tell he felt it too. For the remainder of the conference we partnered for seminars and cheesy group exercises. He told me about his family back in India; I told him about Nate, the recent hiking trip we had taken to the Yukon. In the evenings, we fed the birds. We drank hot toddies. We talked about the world in which we lived, and the world we imagined for our students.

He once chided me for using the term *late-stage capitalism* because it was impossible to know, he said, which stage we had reached.

'That's not the point,' I said. 'It's not meant to be taken literally, it's more a hashtag mood. When I was a teenager, you couldn't say the word *Capitalist* without people thinking you were a *Communist*. In Grade 10, I had a French teacher who would sashay down the hall in sailor-style bell-bottoms that laced up the front of his crotch, and no one, least of all him, dared use the word *gay*, or even *flamboyant*.

What I mean is that we are better at calling things that live under our noses by their proper names now. And that is a first step.'

I remember the way he looked at me then, like he wanted to call what was happening between us by its proper name, and that he knew what it would mean if he tried.

In bed at night I longed for him so powerfully, it was possible I levitated above the quilt painstakingly assembled in small-town Ontario church basements. It was lust I felt, without a doubt, but it was seldom relieved when I slipped my hands under that quilt and swallowed the sounds of my own pleasure. My need was for something other and larger than myself.

These days I have thoughts like *It is very disappointing that plastic wrap is bad for the environment, because it is* so *useful.*

It is true that when the pain comes and empties me out, I imagine Devin next to me in that backyard outside of time. But I know it is a shining single moment in my day-to-day, an evanescent escape only.

BREATHE

LOCKDOWNS WE HAVE KNOWN by ENG4U1-03

Once my dad came to bring me my lunch in Grade 4 and didn't check in at the office. Miss O'Neill called it when she saw him peering into the tiny windows in classroom doors. Also, he was wearing too-short sweatpants and his shoes had holes. Because he is an 'artist.' Once a man held two people hostage in the apartment building behind the football field. There were snipers in the parking lot. We weren't supposed to open the blinds, but we could see it all through the bottom bit of the window. Live eye. Apparently, he hit his mother but didn't shoot her. Once we were locked down for three hours because Jasper's friend wrote a story about bringing a machete to school because he was pissed off at his math teacher for not letting him rewrite a test. Once some skinny-ass bitch came at my cousin in the courtyard. She had a blade and she was hella good at fighting. Once I lost it on this asshole who said he fucked my girl. I said I had a pistol in my locker. I didn't. But my mom has one in the freezer. She thinks I don't know. Once they shot Jevon's brother right out front. Like it was nothing. Once Alastair told Brandi told Carmen told Nate told Rachel told Vincent told Bridget told Chris told Mohammed told Matt that Saul had a gun in his bag. And the teachers believed us because they had to. Once we were locked down for almost four hours and Stella had a seizure and hit her head and had a concussion and still can't remember the name for the sweet, sticky yellow-orange fruit that is so good in smoothies. Mango. It's a mango. Once my boyfriend who was expelled (not really, 'safe schools transfer') came back and stabbed someone he had beef with and no one ever asked me afterward how I felt. I was shook and sad and it was partly my fault and we broke up and also I loved him. Once these six Grade 10 kids said Mr. Sanders, the guidance counsellor, was a racist (he is a racist) and they ran into the VP's office all bigged up with righteousness and people (adults) felt unsafe so the hall monitor herded them out and the secretary locked the door and then: LOCKDOWN. Once there was a shooter in the immediate area and first they said HOLD AND SECURE, just go about your business but don't leave, but then they said LOCKDOWN because he had been spotted (maybe?) at the east entrance.

FADUMA

I can see that Miss is losing it. She's pretending she can still be in charge but obvi that is completely false. There is a reason people always want me in their group when we have to 'collaborate'. I am super-good at keeping things in order and making sure stuff gets in on time. It's partly just that I have a system with my markers and day planner but it's also my personality type/learning style, which Mr. Garmond, the psych teacher, says is not a thing anymore, but whatever, it is a thing.

Shai-Anna has started to make a little soft place in the corner. People are just throwing her their sweatshirts and cute cardigans and some kids have swimming stuff, so towels too. I know this thing will be controlled by Miss's body even if her mind is kind of preoccupied or vacant. Ryan is still watching her like it's his only job, which it is, but if you ask me he's a bit too in on the task. I guess it's good, though; that's a big thing for doctors and nurses – vigilance. You have to be like a soldier or a good Muslim. Still, I think an occasional update is necessary so I scoot over to where he's sitting.

'Ryan?' I tap him on the shoulder. 'Can you tell us when she's having one? I'll get Mark to write it on the board, then we'll all know.'

I signal Mark across the room, tap at my wrist, mime some letters with my hand in the air.

Mark meets my eyes, nods seriously. So. Hot.

Ryan looks superscared. Maybe because I've asked him to time *and* talk? 'Just give me a signal – like hold up your hand, okay?'

Miss, who has been listening, nods too, then makes this sort of strange face like she's about to tell a bad joke or apologize. 'Faduma?' she says.

'Yeah, Miss? How can I help?'

'I really need to pee. Like, really.'

Oh no. 'Shai-Anna,' I hiss.

She doesn't hear me or is ignoring me, which would be insensitive considering the predicament we are in.

'Shai-Anna,' I say again, a bit more loudly. She looks up at me and gives me this really mean look like I am interrupting a queen in the middle of royal negotiations or something.

'What,' she mouths obnoxiously.

'Miss has to pee!' I try to match her obnoxiousness but instead I just end up saying it too loud and now the whole class knows Miss's business. As if they didn't already, I guess, but still.

'Fuck,' says Shai-Anna. 'We're gonna need a toilet corner.' She stands up as she says this and puts her hands on her hips. Her Jamaican accent is getting stronger too and it's not like she's putting it on like some of the Caribbean girls do when they're playing or dancing, imitating their mothers or aunties or some dancehall star. It's actually for real and it feels bossy but true. Like she is a leader. Our leader.

ELISE

Faduma is staring at me, open-mouthed.

Well, okay, but she needs to know that this is what it's like being pregnant, giving birth – all of the inside stuff – blood, piss, shit, organs even – become somehow outside. If not on public view, at least more present and obvious. And now? Whatever modicum of modesty, of decency I might have clung to has left me. I gotta piss like a racehorse, my dad used to say when he came home after a night at the Legion, and it wasn't until I actually saw a racehorse piss that I grasped the aptness of this analogy. I had understood racehorses to be prone to skittishness, with spindly legs and large gentle eyes – Black Beauties all. But when they pee, it is thunderous, it is with urgency and intention. So it will be with me, my baby sitting like a sandbag on my bladder. I try a trick. I let a little bit out – like bleeding a rad – to relieve the pressure. The relief is momentary, but then another contraction comes and I grab onto Ryan, who looks like he might throw up when he feels the force of my grip. Still, he presses the buttons on his device and lifts his hand to Faduma, who nods to Mark, who glances up at the clock and writes the time on the board. My eyes fill with tears of gratitude before the contraction takes me completely. When it subsides, I squeeze Ryan's hand again and then wet myself thoroughly.

'Faduma,' I say, and look down at my crotch. 'Too late.'

'Oh, Miss,' she says. 'It's okay.'

But I am not embarrassed. I know this is the least of it. Then Shai-Anna is by my side.

'We must get these pants off you,' she says.

I nod meekly.

Shai-Anna looks up at the rest of the students. 'Our job now is to keep Miss dry and comfortable. Do you understand? If you cannot help, you must stay quiet and out of the way. If you do not like blood and are freaked out by a screaming, moaning, half-naked woman, you must put your earbuds in your ear holes and turn the volume way the fuck up. Do you understand? And if that motherfucker who is out there tries anything, we must keep Miss safe, we must keep each other safe. Do you *understand*?'

I am proud of Shai-Anna and also a little intimidated by her. I think she will make a fine midwife. The other students are silent, although some of them nod in assent. Some just roll their eyes. But no one objects to Shai-Anna's bid for power, her imperious chin jerks and general's stance. I suspect they, like me, are a little bit in awe of her.

I read, just this morning, an essay on *Othello* that described Shakespeare's M.O. as being an exercise in exploring human nature 'on the very verge of its confine.' I think that is where we find ourselves now. I am not unaware of the potential for drama in the situation. And Shai-Anna? An outsider destined to win acclaim and honours, the stripes and medals? What would happen, I wonder, if we gave facilitators of life, rather than makers of war, their due? If we trained our spotlight beyond just Shakespeare's sister. Onto Shakespeare's mother's midwife instead! *My parts, my title, and my perfect soul / Shall manifest me rightly.*

SHAI-ANNA

Foolish woman. How does she think she's going to get through this without some true expert support? I feel my granmumma speaking through me. They are not subsiding, the contractions. That baby is coming. And I can see what is needed maybe clearer than I've ever seen anything in the whole of my life. Faduma will be useful. She's got that good-girl need to please. Plus Miss seems to trust her for some reason. And Ryan? He'll do as he's told. The rest of them? As long as they don't get in the way or bring their own hang-ups into the mix. The birthing zone looks like the bottom of a hamster cage. But we will make do. *Heel nevah go before toe.*

'I need to check your dilation,' I say. And I see Miss's face change from game for this to WTF. Because there is a difference between having a student cheerlead you and having her fingers up inside your pumpum. Boundaries is a thing people talk about a lot these days and I think we're gonna fuck them up real good. There's a kid slouched down over by the corner of the desk – I think his name's Joseph.

'Ryan,' I say. 'Get that kid to throw over the hand sanitizer.'

Ryan nudges the guy with his foot and points to the bottle. The kid reaches up, then lobs it easily at me, as if it is the most natural thing in the world. I wonder what it costs him, to look that cool all the time. I fumble the catch a little but make up for it by moving right into the pump and rubbing my hands together professionally. I get Faduma to pass me a water bottle, then dribble a little over my hands for good measure. Technically, it should be up to my elbows and a good four-minute scrub. *But beggahs can't be choosahs.* I fold a couple of sweatshirts and slide them under Miss's butt. Her knees are already up, but I get her to widen them a bit more and peel off her panties. She is facing the side blackboard for modesty, but I can tell Faduma is starting to freak the fuck out. She is staring at me all wide-eyed.

'It doesn't arrive with a stork or on a cloud. This shit is real and X-rated.'

She nods. Like she knew all along.

'Is this good, Shai-Anna?' says Miss.

She is leaning back, offering herself up to me. I feel some … tenderness toward her. But I need to be the opposite of tender. I need to be strong. My mother speaks over my granmumma. *Insert fingers palm up and angle toward the anus. The cervix is the end of the vaginal canal.* I crouch down to meet Miss's eyes.

'You ready?'

She nods and closes her eyes.

Her vulva is pink and huge – unlike anything I have ever seen. *Stop gawkin', gyal, and do your job*. I slide my fingers in and feel her wince and tense.

'It's okay,' I say. 'Breathe.' But the truth is I am suddenly terrified. I have no clue what I'm doing. My fingers stuck up inside this white woman. My teacher! Then I feel it. Two fingers fit easily, three will work, and four snugly. Four centimetres dilation. I slide my fingers out and feel her relax.

'You're having a baby, Miss Foster. It's happening.' She looks at me with surprise and maybe some kind of faith, like she is delivering herself over.

SAM

I watch the bottle of hand sanitizer, a translucent silvery oblong with an aquamarine label, arc up and out of the boy's hand and it makes me ache so profoundly that I almost regret what I have done. The force and casual intent, the feel of the moulded plastic in his hand, the electrical contraction of tricep and the feathery letting go from fingers once confidently clasped. I yearn for it. To be in a body, to bid a body, without noting the bidding, to be earthbound and boyish and sure. The bottle is suspended there – in the rarefied atmosphere of room 108 – having been summoned by the bossy one, Shai-Anna. I recognize her, although not like this, with this ... what is it they call it? Gravitas, this solidity and wisdom. I picked the wrong time to leave, maybe. But still I am here to witness this, a last slowing down and admittance, a gift visited upon me. And now the bottle arcs past the hijabi girl, who tilts her lovely chin up to watch. It is Shai-Anna who reaches her hand up and completes the parabola, the airborne story. Then it is all go and bustle – what is it the Shakespeareans say? Hither and yon. Yawn and shiver. Hare Krishna. Krishna Hare. And now the teacher, the one they are tending, she is facing the hijabi, clutching her by the forearms, telegraphing something through the beams that emanate from her hooded pale blue eyes – that she is scared, that she is sorry, that she is urgent with life. These are things I know without knowing, sense without source or effort. Not because I am dying, but because I wanted so badly to live and cannot.

MARIA

I knew it was important to keep lines of communication open with Anthony's mother, but I also knew the level of antipathy I felt toward her – she existed for me like most of the teachers at the school, a form of oblivious adult who moved like a cipher through the students' lives. That we were all part of the same fucked-up system was insultingly obvious to me. Still, my allegiances had been set. I was Team Anthony in my heart. So when she contacted me to set up an appointment, I sensed I would have to work hard to understand this woman's world.

The outer shell – the show of it – I was confident in. The rest – my ability to listen deeply – I doubted. And I knew that if I didn't find a chink in my shell through which to love her, just a little, I would be of no help to either of them.

I shook her hand and met her eyes. She had dark hair like mine, a hint of light moustache on her upper lip. Her body was compact and fleshy. She wore a scarf I admired, despite myself. She smelled like a body wash I had used in my twenties and for a second I was there: picking up part-time shifts in a group home by day, crashing on futons next to people as wanton and joyful and lost as me by night.

'Maria,' I said. 'Maria Almada.'

'Ah, Portuguese,' she said. Her eyes flickered with recognition. And maybe dismay?

'Brazilian lite,' I said. 'My grandfather. I still love sardines and cheer for Ronaldo. But I have no Portuguese.'

She laughed. 'I get it. My mother's Portuguese, but I lost the language – and the pride, really – to WASPy schooling. I'm Lucy.'

Uh-oh. I just needed to understand her. I didn't want to like her. 'So,' I said. 'Sit, please.'

She pulled off her purse and placed it on the table beside us, her eyes skimming over the jar of condoms, pausing only briefly. Okay, so there would be no anti-sex evangelism to deal with; she was hip to what the kids were up to. Or at least she wanted me to think she was.

I took a deep breath. My head was pounding and my mouth was dry. I had forgotten to take my prophylactic dose of Advil before I fell into bed the night before, sore from dancing, fuzzy-minded from vodka coolers, a cheeky line of cocaine. Mini-epiphany: I had not travelled far from the strangers' futons of my youth.

'Water?' I said, and filled two mugs for us from the water cooler in the corner without waiting for her answer. The jug glugged loudly. We watched as the air bubble inside rose and burst.

'I'm glad you came.' I smiled professionally.

'Yes,' Lucy said. 'I know that Anthony … He's always been … ' She stopped to search for something in her purse. 'I found this.' She was holding a piece of paper folded carefully in thirds. The paper was a creamy ivory colour, of the kind you'd find in an expensive sketchbook. 'It's Anthony's. I know. I mean I know I shouldn't have – ' She held it out to me, then seemed to change her mind. 'Can I read it to you?'

'Does he know you have it?'

She shook her head.

And this was a moment for me, the kind that arrives when your job is to hold other people's stories, and sometimes the stories you hold exist inside other stories or nudge up against each other, and you have to decide if you have the right to enter the stories at all.

'How do you think he'd feel about you reading it to me?' Beyond the mandated ethics, the regulations, there was something more pulsing and real than all the healthy boundaries I had set, for which I had been taught to stand guard, like a sentinel.

Lucy was having none of it. 'For fuck's sake.' She banged the letter down flat onto the desk between us. 'He'd be pissed off of course.'

There it was. I could see Anthony in her now, or her in Anthony. It was a relief to feel the connection in this way; it made me feel better for what I was about to do.

'Read it to me, then.' She needed my permission and I gave it.

Lucy's hands were in her lap, the letter set upon them as if it had just fallen there by chance. She met my eyes and nodded. 'I found it on his desk. It fell out when I moved some books. I was just going to clean up a bit – I thought it was something that belonged in his binder. Just some random notes. But it wasn't from his binder. It didn't belong with his notes. It's addressed to his friend Sam … ' She waited for me to acknowledge Sam, their connection, my complicity in the friendship.

I considered impassivity, a wide-eyed innocence, but quickly dismissed this. I had opened the door. I nodded.

She waved the paper at me and unfolded it. 'It starts *Yo, yo, Sam* and then a winky emoji.' She winked big, like a clown, and I smiled.

Then she swallowed and I thought how beautiful and how like her son she was when she was holding something in.

'So this was when I should have stopped, folded the paper back in on itself, let it stay safe and unseen. But I didn't. I didn't because I am his mother and some part of me thinks I have the *right*. I have heard and believe that this is wrong, that children must, at some point, find their own way … But, I mean, I used to wash his every crevice, you know? I knew every part of him. How could I not know now?' She pulled at her earlobe, something I had seen Anthony do, then seemed to come back to herself, her purpose. She cleared her throat, then began to read.

'*I need you to know something about me but when I tell you, when you read this – it is possible we won't be us anymore. If I were you I'd be afraid of me. I'd shun me.*' She looked up at me, away from the letter. 'I thought, that's it, he's finally going to declare his love for that odd damaged girl. And my heart went out to him and the way he always, always misses the mark. And I wondered whether this was something he had learned from me or his father or some fucked-up alchemy of the two of us. Always a half-step off, just behind the beat, never quite the same frequency, wrong place, right time, right place, wrong time, you know?'

I nodded. It wasn't my place to offer anything at this point. And this was uncharted territory for me too – so many unknowns. Were we in therapy or in conversation? My professional self seemed to have distanced herself, stationed like a Valkyrie in my peripheral vision. Lucy picked up the letter again.

'*But maybe, maybe, you can forgive me, because you know about the way sharp things – wielding them – can bring relief. Okay, Sam, okay. So, I have some thoughts, right? And you've told me enough of yours that I know thoughts are not always the sum total of a person's game. I get that. But these thoughts are fucking with me, making me think I'm the type of person who would do really fucked-up, evil things. And JFC, I don't want to lose you, but I feel like if I don't tell someone I'm gonna bust open or just fucking lose control. And I am so scared of losing control.*'

Her voice wavered a little here, and I resisted the urge to reach out to her. I nodded again, mutely.

'*How can I even live when I don't trust myself? I have bloody thoughts, Sam. Like not bad dreams, or flashbacks to horror movies, but actual wilful thoughts where I am an actor in the thoughts.*' She stopped. 'Then he quotes a Leonard Cohen line from *Various Positions*, in pretty heavy rotation at our house. You a fan?'

I am a bit taken aback by the incongruity of this question but I nod again even though I can't stand Cohen, the gloom and almost-singing, so many years of silent retreat when the world seems always to be calling out for people like him, the wise ones, to speak up and give us something to hang on to …

'Yeah, he's genius. Although maybe not a great soundtrack for teenagehood, right?' She turns back to the letter. '*I wonder sometimes about the aftermath, bloodbath aftermath, all those school killers who made it out alive. Were the visions, the dreams … Were they gone or did they persist? Because if I were to … Sam … If I were to … do something about these thoughts and they were still there? I couldn't face it anymore so might it not be better to just shortcut it to suicide? To make the only blood spilt my own? Imagine if the Macbeths had short-circuited all that mayhem? Not such a great story but a lot less blood, right?'*

Lucy stopped to look at me, found my gaze with her own. 'What do you do? What would you do? This is my son! He is of my body. He is my body.' She was not crying, but her anguish, its depth and terrible clout, was there in her voice. She took a deep breath and continued. '*I dunno if this is the right thing to say to you and I probably won't give this to you but you need to know that if I'm gone I never did it to hurt you. It was to protect them. And I know we don't often put a lot of stock into what they think of us. I know we are different, but shit, we have to live in this world too, don't we?*' She took a deep breath; I could see the effort in it.

'That's it,' she said. 'That's the end. He ends with a rhetorical question. Only I want to answer his question for him. I want to be the answer to his question! But I can't, can I?' She began to cry now, messily, the tears seeming to come not just from her eyes but from the pores in her face, everywhere at once. I passed her a tissue and swallowed my own tears, which had gathered in my throat, waiting.

'No,' I said. 'No, you can't.'

ELISE

I breathe deeply – feel it down in my lower ribs, then in my guts, compressed as they are, up against my lungs and heart. I am scared. Scared that I can't manage this no matter my surroundings, scared that my body won't manage it, and then just scared by the fact of it barrelling toward me. There is no stopping now, literally no way to halt the triggering hormones and waves of convulsions and expulsions. *Nate, where are you?*

I wave to Ryan.

'Another one?' he says.

'No. I need you to get me my phone.'

'Uh, we're not supposed to use our phones in a lockdown, Miss.'

I stare at him.

'Okay,' he says. 'Which drawer?'

'Right-hand side, second one down. Quickly, before the next one comes.'

He scurries over in an awkward army crouch, slides open the drawer, then holds up the device for my approval.

Jesus, now they all know what I'm up to. 'Bring it over,' I hiss. And, oh shit, here comes another one ...

SHAI-ANNA

I was five when I went to Jamaica for the first time and began to understand something about my mumma and how she fit and didn't fit in her home. My granmumma's house was not a shack exactly, but it had elements of that, a closeness to the earth that felt dirty and unfinished to me. She was the most wrinkled woman I had ever seen, and when she squatted in her garden I used to think it was where she went to sleep at night, upright and stuck in the land.

One morning she roused me from my bed, passed me a slice of mango, and said, 'Come, child, there's something for you to see. City chile nevah seen where life come from.'

Out behind the vegetable garden, next to a broken-down shed, a dog was lying on its side and at first I thought it was dead and I held tight then tighter to my granmumma's hand because I wanted her to know I understood and she didn't have to show me and I didn't want her to let me go and I wanted to be back in my bed. I believed then that Jamaica was a place populated with more ghosts than the rest of the world, duppies and spirits and ghouls. It was a haunted-story place, woven out of tales and sayings that had no real standing in the larger world of my school back home in my city of Toronto. But as we got closer, there was this smell, a smell I connect now with new life spilling out into the world, and there were morning life noises – squawking birds and chirruping tree frogs.

My granmumma bent down to lay her hand on the dog's flank. 'She is quiet now, restin', but don't you worry, she will bring forth a racket of noise with her babies,' she whispered.

ELISE

Once it has passed, I look down at the phone I have been squeezing in my palm. The screen is black and shiny and for a moment I see myself reflected, but then I press the power button and up pops Joey peering over his dad's shoulder at me. It is an old picture, taken when he was only three and not yet savvy when it came to selfies and sartorial choices. Nate's head – the balding back of it – and his hand are in it too. Joey is at the tail end of a laugh; he is coming back to himself after a bout of hilarity. Prompted by what? A knock-knock joke or a dropped sock, one of his dad's exaggerated *say what?* faces. It doesn't matter. It's that discovery of the world's absurdity in its many forms that I find so appealing. Of all the firsts, the notion that one's surroundings can be strange and surprising and often comical is the one that I value the most. Hang on to it, I think. It will bolster you when misery and misunderstanding come knocking.

I enter my pattern on the screen and watch another image emerge, a landscape in Georgian Bay, sun on rocks, trees, water. I have texts and emails – little square icons stacked in the corner. Of course I do. And, for once, I don't feel immediately compelled to tap on them, to see what missives they hold. Not while I'm here. It seems sacrilegious almost, to burst our fragile bubble, superimposed, forced as it may be. Still, there are the two of them to consider, roaming around on the outside. My boys. I click on the texts first. A reminder from my dentist. It has been over six months since my last cleaning. An offer to upgrade my data plan. And three texts from Nate. 1. *Can you pick up that butter chicken sauce and some red peppers?* 2. *I heard there's a lockdown happening at the school – everything ok?* 3. *Haven't heard from you school still locked down? text me please.* The run-on, the lower case, and the *please* are signs he is feeling ruffled. His is not a mind that plays on the edges of disaster like mine, which means that when trauma and heartbreak do inevitably occur he is deeply shocked, but he lives the rest of his days skating over the thin ice that keeps us on the upside of cold, wet despair. The *please* means he is actually worried. It cracks my heart open. I have so little control. But he has less – I can't bear the thought of him careening into panic. *All good,* I type back quickly, then stop to breathe through the seizing cramps in my legs, *I'm sure it will be lifted soon.* Like I have some inside intel he does not. *How's Joey?* Like I am not about to bring forth Nate's progeny in the company of a bunch of seventeen-year-olds, next to a recycling bin and a poster illustrating the best way to ask Level 4 Higher Order Thinking questions. Nate's response is swift: *He's good. Eating french fries.*

Joey is a sturdy fellow, more solid at seven than he was at eight months when my breast milk and his newly discovered passion for Baby Mum-Mum crackers had conspired to make him sumo wrestler-like in appearance. He is not chubby now, not exactly, but he has a physical presence, a substance I admire. A confidence too. He does not, like other children I have observed in playgrounds, on sidewalks, in supermarkets, scream and cry fat tears if he falls or stumbles, if another kid shoves or taunts him. Instead, he springs up, and when again upright, scans his surroundings before proclaiming to whatever audience is in earshot: I'm okay, I'm OKAY! So, not only is he – in diction that has become cliché, a worn-out receptacle for all of our efforts as educators – *resilient,* but he also wants to reassure concerned caregivers. Considerate, confident, resilient fellow.

Still, I know not to get smug about this. We emerge into every stage of our children's lives armed only with what has come before, then look up, blinking and stunned, at what they have become. We gamely adapt, then blithely forget. We try to prepare. It is de rigueur to be on the lookout for a child's exceptionality, to celebrate their difference – and why not? We are all so specific and wonderfully strange. Joey's thing, we agree, is his sweetness and unflappability. Is he smart? Hard to tell. He is himself.

When we asked him what he would like to show his little sister when she arrives, he furrowed his dear little brow before replying. 'The place with the good food and furniture.'

'The museum?' We had spent many dreamy, dull afternoons there, wandering through dinosaur skeletons and gemstones, finding our place in the expensive but well-stocked cafeteria. There were buttons to press, intricate ships sailing endlessly behind glass, grinning taxidermied foxes, and delicate dead birds in tiny oblong drawers. The boxes of dress-up clothes had been well-pawed by other children and their obliging mothers.

'No,' he said, shaking his head in consternation. 'Not that place. There are rugs there. And lamps. Beds all in a row.'

'Ikea,' Nate said. 'He's talking about Ikea.'

So this is our culture. And we have embraced it. Most Saturdays we follow the arrows through the well-appointed rooms, the bins of brightly coloured stuffies and kitchen utensils, the plants and posters. Sometimes, when Joey runs ahead, entranced by a squishy sofa or a bunkbed with stairs, I will duck into one of the tiny studio apartments, stare at a blank TV, marvel at the Swedish space-saving shelving, transport myself into a life where useful objects only ever have one welcoming home.

'Yes,' says Joey. 'I will show her Ikea.'

'Have we failed?' I ask Nate.

'No,' he says. 'Probably. Hard to say.'

That fatalism that is part reassurance, part provocation.

'We should encourage his passions?' he says, and smiles – at me or at himself?

He is an asshole, but he is my asshole.

GUSH

SHAI-ANNA

Miss is busy with her phone and for a flash I feel sorry for her – yearning for her people. I pick up her bloodied underwear and a moist paper towel and place them in the tiny garbage can. When I look up, a boy is staring at me from the sidelines. He's white but also a bit green around the gills. And I realize it must be the blood and the moaning. I nod at him fiercely. I wonder why we have always sent men into battle, when it is women who truly know blood.

I was at home, thank God, when I got my period for the first time. It was early – I was only ten – but Mumma had already explained the basics of it to me, pointed out the box of maxi-pads in the cupboard under the sink, said something else about 'plugs' I might want to use when I got older, made a gesture with her index finger like she was stoppering a hole between her legs. But she was out cleaning when it happened. I had been watching cartoons – *The Magic School Bus*. I was too old for the show but it was easy. It passed over and through me as I sat on the couch with a plate of scrambled eggs propped on my lap. I was pushing them around, making little mounds, thinking how I could camouflage them under last night's leftovers in the garbage because we *do not waste* in my household. My belly was queasy, like something was capsizing in there. And on the screen, that magical white lady was leading them all in that bus into a river where the bus turned into the body of a salmon fighting its way upstream. I thought of the one where they'd journeyed through Ralphie's veins and his white blood cells attacked the bus, thinking it was an invader. I'd dreamed about that episode later, and when I woke up I felt scared and excited. Like there were possibilities that went along with understanding things. But this day the magical lady – Ms. Frizzle was her name – took the kids to the desert and her journey made me feel a strange sadness. I put my plate of eggs on the couch beside me and I didn't even have the energy to move it to the kitchen even though I knew there'd be hell to pay if I didn't scrape and scrub it clean. Then it was like I peed without meaning to, or something just spilled out of me, and when I went to the bathroom to check, there was a rusty red cloud just sitting there in my panties. And I had a feeling that was the opposite of the feeling the magic school bus had given me, like the possibilities in life were just fantasies, cartoons that could be shut down with a point and a click.

I was eight years old the first time I saw a human baby being born. We were in my auntie Patrice's living room. We were all gathered around the TV, watching some nonsense, maybe a reality show, yes, that was it. *The Bachelor.* And Auntie Patrice said her back was paining her and we all ignored her 'cause she always had some reason for griping and carrying on and this pregnancy had been the worst for that according to my mother who was not the biggest fan of Auntie Patrice to begin with, mostly because she had ignored her advice about papaya enzymes and insisted instead that ice cream was the only true cure for heartburn. 'She's never gonna lose them pounds,' my mumma said, and sucked her teeth long and hard.

And then it was the rose ceremony and we shushed each other to hear which of the ladies would be blessed, and Auntie Patrice said, 'Uuuhhh, uuuhhh, my back is paining me something fierce,' and she squatted right down in front of me so I had to scramble up onto my knees to see what was actually happening with the rose ceremony. Then Patrice just went and peed all over my mumma's new wall-to-wall.

'Lord help me,' said my mumma. 'Her water just broke all over my carpet.'

'Call Jordan,' my cousin Collette said. 'I think she needs to go to the hospital.'

I'm ashamed to say I was still trying to see who would be the chosen few who found their way into the bachelor's heart. I thought, that's right, Jordan, take this nuisance moaning auntie away.

Then Auntie Patrice let out this shriek like she'd been stabbed and said, 'NO HOSPITAL IS HAPPENING TODAY. I can feel the child coming.'

And all hell broke loose and people were running around with kettles and towels, and my mumma said, 'Shai, go get the cooking oil,' and I thought, Why does she want to be cooking at a time like this? Nobody thought to turn the TV off but I was quickly losing interest in the bachelor's choices and Patrice was all of a sudden stark naked and moaning like that line from 'Away in a Manger' that says the cattle were lowing – she was naked and lowing much louder than the *Bachelor* and down on all fours with her bottom in the air and I could see her vagina but it didn't look like any other vaginas I'd seen, which was really only my own, my mumma's, my older sister Fiona's, and also Celeste's from swim lessons and she had hair down there that she made me count with her one day in the change room. This vagina was huge and red and when Patrice screamed I saw it pulse open and something hairy peek out. My mumma was down there at Patrice's bottom.

'Alright, girl,' she said. 'Loosen your anus a bit next time.' Then I saw her pour the oil out into her palm and use her fingers to rub it into the crack of Patrice's bottom or kind of behind her vagina. *Vulva and perineum,* came my mumma's voice in my head. *We use the proper names for body parts in my house.* Even though there are definitely lots of other names out there.

That day that Ms. Frizzle swam upstream with the salmon, I met mumma at the door when she got home, her cleaning bag weighting her, making her lopsided. When I told her what had happened, she looked at me with anger, like I had broken something precious, then she drew me in close so I could smell her sweat and coconut hair oil.

'That's it then, child,' she said. 'It is the way of the world.'

She took me by the hand without looking me in the eye and led me to the bathroom, showed me the box again, even though I'd already told her that I had a pad stuck in there like a diaper.

MARIA

Every morning, I count out tiny bright pills, shake them from their squat white bottles. Magnesium for calm, a B complex for stress, C for scurvy, D because we live in the north where sunshine is scarce, fish oil for braininess. I observe them in my palm, my little pile of wellness, oblong and round, tiny and bulbous, and maybe I pray? I don't know. But I put some faith in the vitamin collections, I do. I have, thus far, avoided mainstream pharmaceuticals of the prophylactic or maintenance variety, not because I don't believe in them – because I do – I have seen the difference they can make: the SSRIs, the SNRIs, the NASSAs, the TCAs ... RSVP! ASAP! How hope can be jigged and rejigged, upped, then re-upped to save lives.

It is true, despite what your latest, greatest gluten-free friend might tell you, that some people need those pills to survive. Not because they are broken, no, but because the world is; the world in its everydayness is designed to fillet hope, then sell it back to you in the form of slick gadgets, magical leggings (leggings!), and the promise of fulfillment through gorgeousness, through efficiency, through satiety and sex. I know what we are really craving, whether it be in an oddly reassuring diagnosis in the pages of the *DSM*, the words and touch of a lover, the adoring gaze of a pet, the communal heartbeat of a dance floor. What we want is to feel understood. And maybe this is the crux of it. That to feel understood is not to *be* understood – but the effect? The effect is the same. Do my vitamins make me feel understood? Maybe on some – cellular? – level they do.

And I see the hypocrisy and silliness in my regimen when paired with my late-night fixes of trance and grinding. The exceptions I make for street drugs! Still, these are the risks I am willing to take, the bargains I am willing to strike. What are your trade-offs, I wonder, every time I meet someone new: client, colleague, stranger at a bus stop. How the fuck do *you* manage?

ELISE

I am staring at the cheap dropped ceiling, which has a piss-coloured stain from an ancient leak and is marked also with what looks like graffiti, two blobby letters or symbols, and I am thinking about homes – how strange it is that, like the animals we are, we mark ours with things, our sheddings, and our scents, the collection of strange debris in the desk drawers, years of weird pedagogical sediment, dried-up pens, lip balms, cellphone and extension cords, so many lonely rubrics, the number of times I have written *run-on sentence* or *verb tense consistency* or *use transitions to link your ideas,* the various names on unclaimed and forgotten test papers, the humans who have cycled through this place, then been spit out, dazed and mangled, into the larger world. When they come back to visit, their faces alight with expectation, eager to tell of the ways their lives forked and fell or flew, how they were full of triumph or sorrow, I call them *honey,* or *kid,* endearments designed to conceal the fact that their names have fled my consciousness. And they seem not to care. *Do you remember me, Miss?* They are so happy to remind me that my forgetting seems incidental, benign.

My gaze travels down the wall to a *Midsummer Night's Dream* poster from the 1980s, mortals and fairies cavorting in shades of turquoise and dreamy greens, fairies that live behind boulders or sit stalwart in ancient streams, the nooks that form at the base of oak trees, fairies that protect the forests and curse meddling humans with infertility or beastly features. I love the fairies for their obliviousness to human custom. I suspect they beat their children, tear pacifiers from their tiny lips, and ignore their plaintive cries. Fairies are not good mothers. They have read none of the parenting books or blogs; their babies' cribs are full of pokey twigs and mossy clumps. They go out dancing at bedtime, leaving their wee ones in the care of belching bullfrogs. They throw the guts of raspberries to the toddlers they have imprisoned in jails fashioned of reeds and sticky tree sap.

Oh, but they are so joyful! When they deign to lift their offspring into wild embraces, it is as if tiny diamonds fly from their outstretched arms. And the comfort they provide to a weeping wee one is as fresh and crystal clear as the water that runs from a hidden mountain well. It enters the heart and stays there as refuge and reserve to be accessed with a blink and a sigh. They are loving in their own way.

I am thinking all of these things when I feel it, my water breaking, the surge of liquid between my legs. Different from menstruation, although not entirely, the volume of liquid larger, but the lack of control, the surge and gush, the same.

With Joey I thought I'd peed the bed, had to bend down to sniff the patch of sheet I had been sitting on, roused by my bulk's preparatory rumblings. It was the beginning and end of everything, of the time I would spend yoked to my baby, of the true yoking to another. Practice for the dissolution of the self that happens quite literally on day three after the baby's birth. The midwives called it the Leaky Day, breasts rock-hard and seeping, eyes squirting tears, womb still bleeding from the birth, that soft cushion of uterus lining finding its way out on a tide of hormones.

My heart thumps like a mad racehorse in my chest. My baby has lost her protection, her cushion against the outside. I want badly to hold her in, to keep her safe and contained. And I know this cannot be; my job now is to encircle her until the circle pinches like too-small jeans, then release her again and again into whatever the world manifests. There will be no moving now. My body will not allow it.

'Shai-Anna,' I say weakly. 'My water has broken.' Why the present perfect? A declaration.

She stares into my eyes. It seems we truly recognize each other for the first time.

'Okay,' she says. 'Okay.'

SHAI-ANNA

I returned every morning of those two weeks at my granmumma's to check on the puppies. The morning air was not like Canada air – it woke me up with a shake and a stroke, a *C'mon up an outta sleep cuz there things I need to show yuh.* The mumma and puppies were hunkered down in a lean-to, not much more than a tent if a tent was made of tin and bits of cardboard, some stray wooden shingles. Granmumma had placed old blankets and bits of rag in there too. She had a nest, that mumma dog; she had shelter. And people to care for her.

I was crouching down near to the puppies, my nose almost to the ground, when I heard a shuffle-type sound from behind, and for a second, because I had been thinking about Ms. Frizzle from *The Magic School Bus* as if she was my actual teacher, imagining the approving smile and nod that would greet my discovery, I thought that the teacher had travelled across the ocean to see me, that she cared that much. So the boy who appeared in my orbit instead was a surprise, and not a nice one. I didn't want to share the puppies. The boy stared at me. He was joined to a large branch that he was dragging like a pet. He was my age maybe, although not as tall. He looked toward the mumma dog's lean-to.

'May I see dem?'

Now that he had spoken I recognized him. Not through his voice, but through the shape his face made as he spoke. He was one of the cluster of people who had come to gawk when I first arrived, the celebrity from Canada. He had laughed at my accent with the others, made me repeat words, then whole phrases. They teased me, him and his friends (brothers?), but I knew – how did I know? – that the teasing was a way of putting me in my place. They thought I was better than them. It was not a feeling I was used to, superiority. It made me feel shy and glowy. And also: What would they do if they found out the truth? I had a secret and maybe a power. I made the decision to hold on to it.

'Can I see dem?' he said again.

I shook my head no.

The boy seemed unsurprised, prepared even. He gestured toward the branch he was dragging.

'This is Bob,' he said. 'I'm Adio. You could help me take him to the Place if yuh let me see the puppies.' He gave Bob a sly look. He seemed so confident in the appeal of his barter that I agreed to his terms without thinking. He was less impressed than I expected when he met the pups, nudging a straggler toward the mumma's teat, pointing out a mottled white one as if I had failed to notice its difference. 'Where'll they go after this?'

I shook my head. It was as if he had asked where I was going next, and how could I respond when the answer was automatic, elsewhere, outside my scope? I hadn't thought that far ahead/beyond. Home, I guessed. Home.

'Maybe I could get one,' he said, but he seemed unconvinced. 'Come, let's get Bob back where he belongs.'

I helped him drag the branch, a hover-drag that stirred up dust and dirt along the mountain path. I did not tell anyone I was going; it didn't seem necessary, or at least not important. Bob's home, or Adio's fort, was about ten minutes away by foot – possibly closer, as we were slowed by Bob's lack of legs. It was similar to the dog's lean-to in construction, although the jungle canopy made for a broader, taller roof and bright dabs of green light. Adio lay Bob down, propping the branch up on a boulder.

'There,' he said, pleased with himself. He swept his hand broadly, proudly, in a wide arc. 'Welcome.' I understood then that Bob had just been an excuse for Adio to show me his place. I felt something like fear, something like curiosity, pinch at me. Did he think he could keep me here? But then I saw from his nervous pride that he did not think that possible, that he just wanted the power of my visit, the fanciness of it. He thought I was a queen, Canadian royalty. He pointed to an upside-down Coca-Cola crate. 'Yuh can sit,' he said.

I often saw myself, after that, through Adio's eyes, and wondered how he would respond, how I might disappoint or bewitch him. I knew he would think so much was beneath me – the boys I chased, the girls I fought, the looks I absorbed on the street.

And now? As I crouch next to my teacher, I feel the swell of my capability rising and I wonder again about how I might look caught in Adio's gaze. I know that he would refuse to cheer me on or give me go-girl props. He would consider this unnecessary; he already knew this thing about me. He met my power before I even knew it existed.

EXPAND

FADUMA

My whole self expands outward and I see us all here not from above but from within – as if my body is the room, and the room is my body. My classmates, my teacher, the desks and chairs and backpacks all crowded into this space. The dusty textbooks, the old-school AV equipment, the radiators and stapled-up projects from two years ago on *The Functions of the Family* ('Whose job is love?'). Then there is a whooshing non-sound, and I am next door to it all, apart. It is like the time in Grade 3 when the teacher, Ms. Fedchuk, asked Justin Samuels for his address and he said: 273EllisCourtToron-toOntarioCanadaTheEarthTheSolarSystemTheUniverse – all in one magnificent exhaled breath and I thought he was maybe the coolest kid I had ever met. I thought he must be in touch with his core Muslim, to be so cleverly aware of his place in the world. And now, in this moment, hurling back from my body, this building, and recognizing that there is something larger that is holding me.

When I come back, I see Shai-Anna differently. She is somehow part of me but also entirely herself. I watch her, her hands on her hips, which are held in her tight black leggings, the white leather Jordans and oversized red school hoodie. Her eyelashes are fake but not too ridiculous. She looks good. She catches me checking her out and smiles – by mistake? No, I think she knows her audience.

I wonder why it is necessary to keep Miss's secret from the outside world. Although, weirdly, I want to; it feels correct. I don't understand the logic behind the decision but have accepted it because Shai-Anna said it like she meant it. With conviction.

I wonder also what my father would do. He has taught me, mostly, to respect the police, that lawlessness – men taking the law into their own hands – is a situation to be avoided at all costs. But the police have no place here, I know, in this corner of our universe, in this instance. And who is he to talk? He was an easygoing parent when I was younger, chill, sending me off to the park or the corner store with my cousins, my cousins' cousins. He said he trusted me to keep myself safe, to return to the family who would always be there, to make my own mistakes and find my own forgiveness.

Except. We were playing tag, hopping and skidding over the rickety playground equipment, when Yusuf hissed at me, 'Is that your … dad?'

I thought it was a ploy, a distraction to keep me from being the last kid standing. I shook my head.

'Over there.' He pointed to the bench on the outskirts of the woodchipped play zone where a man sat, hunched and silent, a newspaper stretched in front of his face like a cartoon spy. It couldn't be. It was so silly. Undignified. And why? When he trusted us to only and always do the right thing?

But it was my father's shoes, the black Reeboks he wore when he went on his daily 'constitutionals.' He had followed us. Did I feel betrayed? Yes. Maybe. A little. Was I not big and strong and smart enough to make it out here alone? Without this embarrassment tailing me? And then I was so ashamed. To think my father an embarrassment when he was my family, a man to be respected and honoured.

Now I think I understand that it was not me he mistrusted but the world, which is unpredictable, and also completely predictable, hostile. How should I behave? I believed Shai-Anna because she had chosen to protect the most vulnerable person in the room in the best way she knew how. And that choice is one I know my father would also make, given the chance or the calling.

ENG4U1-03

Now there is a music to Miss's moans, a rhythm and blues, a rollicking and rudeness. We let them come, the utterances, and they become our walls and wonderment and containment as much as the mortar and brick and stone. So that when she goes a beat too long, when there is an interruption or an odd, elongated pause, we become unsettled in ourselves, we shift and pick at our cuticles, clear phlegm from our throats, fart softly, emit our own quiet groans of despair, because we are used to this now. It is our bubble, our commune, *our class*, and any change, good or bad, is still a disruption, a hard rocking of our shared reality. Do we want to be rescued? What would it mean to be rescued?

MARIA

There is a belief, a practice in my therapy-practising subculture, that involves the recognition and affirmation of different parts of the self – the idea that each person is a loose collection of selves hung together in different formations and clanking, dinging bits depending on the day, the year, the hour. And when we ignore or disparage one or more of these parts or – worse still – deny its existence, it is then that problems arise. It's hard to give each of these parts their due, especially if we've been taught by the world, by our beloveds, that there are parts that don't belong, that don't deserve their place, their little bit of breathing room.

'But,' I tell Anthony, 'there are no bad parts. There are only parts.'

He shrugs and sneers at once. Like I am fucking crazy. And he's right. I have a fucking crazy part and it's possible that lately I haven't been giving that part its due. That it is peeking out at the wrong times, wrong places.

'So I'm wondering, Anthony. What does anger look like for you? Can we speak to your anger maybe?'

He shrugs again. 'Dunno. Is this like some sort of therapy seance?'

I smile. 'I guess.' I wish I had my old Ouija board, can imagine us placing our fingertips lightly, deliberately on its edges, calling our own selves into the room.

'What does anger look like for me?'

He is doing the thing that we do, using the repetition of a question for emphasis, for delay, to indicate indignation or despair. He begins jackhammering his knee, updown, updown, updown, its jittering beat calling words forth.

'We took a road trip once, me and my parents. And on the way, on the highway? My dad had a heart attack. We had to pull over onto the shoulder.'

He stops and looks up at me. 'So weird that they call it that. It's all gravel and limbo and the smell of piss and traces of roadkill.' He shudders. 'I *hate* the shoulder. Only, you know what?'

I shake my head no, even though I do know what. The *what* is the crux of it all.

'It wasn't a fucking heart attack. It was a panic attack.'

He sighs, then actually sneers like a cartoon villain. And I don't like him very much in this moment, not very much at all.

'How could he even do that? We're in a metal box hurtling down a deathway and he decides to freak the fuck out?'

I nod. I do not tell him that people rarely – never – choose to have panic attacks. I suspect he knows this. I suspect he is tired of people, adults, telling him what he already knows. He thinks we have called anger forth but I am pretty sure I can only see sadness. But it is not my place to name his parts.

I wait for his breathing to slow a little, then ask, 'What would you like to say to anger, Anthony?'

He laughs. 'Thank you, I would like to say. Thank you.'

'Yes,' I say. 'What are you thanking anger for?'

'For showing me the truth about my dad.'

'What is the truth about your dad?'

'That he is weak. That he is so fucking weak.'

I am nodding and Anthony is weeping.

How many therapists, counsellors, priests, imams, rabbis, shamans, are sitting like me, in this very position, listening to their client, congregant, faithful devotee, cry out and weep while they nod and nod and nod? Calling up the dead and deprived bits of them, forcing them out into the light. Bearing witness and passing Kleenex. We are an army of sorts, I suppose. Which would make me a soldier? What war?

They come to me in my tiny basement office, windowless but bright with slick, incentivizing posters and fluorescent lights, and they unburden themselves, haltingly or in a run-on rush. Later, they will ignore me in the hallways of course, of course, because what we have shared is too much. It settles awkwardly amidst the shouts and curses and laughter, the clanging of lockers, the *fuck you*s and *love you*s. They want to forget about me. Or: they want to adopt me, make me their own – mother, sister, brother, lover. Sometimes they come just the once, and sometimes they return and return, every day, twice a day, so that I am forced to reject them ever-so-gently, to make room for the other supplicants. And then? Their lives unravel away from me. I hold on to the twine of them for as long as my mind and heart allows and then I let go or I lose track of their winding ways. I rarely hear about the ones who have survived and thrived; they gladly let me go. But: Cyndi who overdosed – and she was doing so well, such a pure spirit! And Malcolm who shot a boy in the face as the price of admission to a gang he thought would love him better than his unhinged blood family, and they did, those other lost boys, they loved him strong and strict and cruel. And Rain, beaten senseless by monsters who could not see their sharp wit and sparkling soul, who saw only their glittering eye shadow and the side-to-side sway of their hips. These stories find their way back to me like dogs trailing their own leashes, giving me a soothsayer's knowledge, however patchy and unreliable, of the fate of my young people, it seems there is a negativity bias at play that feels wise, an evolutionary adaptation to which I should pay heed. Anthony was mine to shepherd – and I recognize my limitations, I do – but I had access, a rare connection. He was mine to lose and I lost him – I let go.

ELISE

My phone vibrates in my hand. It is a text from Nate. He can't find the good potato peeler. There is accusation in the double question mark. I know that he is keeping panic at bay by courting normalcy, that he has no idea that I am in labour, labouring, that it is Labour Day, that everything feels so fucking laborious. It has been two hours thirty-seven minutes. I didn't mean for this to happen.

I wonder if this is my fault. I convinced him to have sex with me last week, one afternoon when he got off early and I had stayed home with a sniffle. The thing with pregnant sex is that everything is flushed and plump and shiny. It's like your genitals put on lip gloss and want to make out all the time. So I made it happen despite my bulk and because of my throbbing – I suppose it's like being a thirteen-year-old boy with the distracting fact of a cock that won't calm down. That I am thinking these thoughts at all – the image of me with my leg jerry-rigged up by my husband's arm while he slides in and out of me, our unborn wedged in my distended belly between us – is testament to the fact that the systems, the great bloated institutions we've built to save us from our animal selves, have loopholes, faulty seams. How do we live and work and play together and still allow for these selves? Perhaps it is the big question of education, which, as everybody knows, is different from the question of school. I wonder if my students can guess what I am thinking, if my thoughts play across my face as I sometimes see theirs when they think I am entranced with my own enthusiasms, the momentum of my own voice, the myriad of ways I find to put the lit in literature. Holla. (I did not sign up for this.)

ANTHONY

Maria always made me rate my emotions on a scale of one to ten, and no matter what number I gave her, I always felt like I was lying, pulling the number out of my ass. Because how do you put your feelings on a line? Sometimes in my head, to try to see things the way she was trying to make me see them, I would imagine the numbers swelling like bubble letters. So that somehow a nine, swollen until it was about to burst, was more meaningful, more painful, than a ten, its number one standing like a soldier, and its zero looking all anorexic and empty. And there were days I couldn't answer, my sadness was so large and dirty that to even try to count it, to contain it, was not only impossible, it felt insulting to the sadness itself, which had its own sensitivities and shape.

Still, I try it, sitting here in the Paper Place. I imagine her sitting across from me, her frown making her eyes squinty and kind. On a scale of one to ten, Anthony, can you rate your anger?

Oh, but my anger feels small and pointy, like a snake's fang. It doesn't course through me like it did sometimes in the before time with my parents – an anger so large I knew I had to move or it would burst like an alien baby through my throat. No, this is anger I hold in my mouth like a razor blade, in reserve. Who is the fang blade for? It seems obvious that it has to be myself. My sadness too – what number? A negative, numbing number.

From outside of all this – of my brain, of my useless body, of the Paper Place, of the school that holds, like a body, its own organisms – had come the sound of sirens, far off, and then closer, crying like wounded animals. The noise had grown and echoed and then stopped. And now they are outside.

There is a window in the Paper Place, small and sealed, high up above my head. I pull some boxes over to the spot below it and build a tower, staggering the boxes to form steps up the side. The task calms me; there is satisfaction in seeing it done.

Well done, nimrod. You've built a little staircase to heaven.

Nimrod? The eighties called; they want their slang back.

What. Ever. Why don't you see what's out there.

Okay.

I climb, one, two, three of my steps, and the structure holds. The sky out the window is blue and cloudless. Like someone has slapped a piece of construction paper up there. Unreal. But down below? A whole mess of people and cars, all looking busy with the crisis. I am the crisis. Three police cars, a police van, an ambulance, a firetruck. Why do the firemen always have to show up in their heavy boots and ridiculous suits? For me. I want to scream at them. I am not the emergency! Sam! Sam is the emergency! But I can't say it; my sadness is choking me, my anger sitting, sharp stone under my tongue.

I found her. I called 911. And then I left like a fucking coward. I didn't even touch the body – that's how I thought of it, as The Body, because of several factors: a) I watched too many CSI franchise shows in my formative years, b) it was probably my fault because how could it not be with all my fucked-upedness, okay, I didn't stab her but I probably dragged her down to my level of twisted despair, and c) she would be so mad at me for thwarting her and I hated it when she was mad at me.

Sam is definitely a beautiful human but she did not look beautiful lying there; she looked broken and ... leaky. There was some puke or bile leaking out of her mouth and trails of crusted, dried tears on her cheeks and her skinny body was leaking breath but like she wished it wasn't. Last year my school banned this book that they made into a show because they said it glamorized suicide. So deeply weird. Like you could dress up suicide in a ball gown, make it sparkle. But the thing with suicide? It just is. Suicide is not a willed action you take; it's like an absence of that. When people feel like she felt … Do you know what I wanted to do? I wanted to somehow gather her up and hold her next to me, put her in my pocket, a baby in a pouch. But I was too scared. And I will never forgive myself for that.

When I got home I found the biggest, sharpest knife I could locate. It was in the carving block, upright and phallic. I pulled it out with my thumb and pointer and dropped it in my backpack. Then I threw up in the kitchen sink, mostly Cheerios and bile. I rinsed and wiped down the sides of the sink with some environmentally friendly cleaner that barely masked the smell with eucalyptus. And I went to school to find Maria.

The door was only partway open. When I nudged it with my sneaker, Maria was on the phone like a CEO. She actually glanced up at me and held one finger in the air as if she was a person with stock portfolios and an overworked assistant. I was so angry, and then so sad. I retched a little, which got her attention. She waved toward the seat and I sat. Then, when she had hung up the phone with a shushing click, she turned toward me like I was the next thing on her list, or maybe the thing that had been inserted into her list without permission. I felt like such an idiot.

Then the bell rang and we sat together waiting for things to calm down, for the last stragglers to skid into class, and something softened. In her? In me? In both of us maybe. And then it all came spilling out, like when you're at the bulk store and you pull the lever and always end up with way too many nuts in your bag. Sam. Finding Sam. Loving Sam. Leaving Sam. The knife in my bag. My skateboard and my backpack and my quick strides through the hallways, past closed classroom doors. To see her – the only adult person who truly knew how disgusting I was, how cowardly and broken. And she had listened, she had.

'The knife,' she said. 'It's in your bag?'

It was.

'And you are angry?'

Of course I was. It was like she was some kind of emotional cavewoman all of a sudden. Or an old-school interrogator. And I saw it, the shift in her eyes. I saw the puppet master in there, the strings that pulled her this way and that. I saw myself in her eyes; how I went from Anthony, Patient, Client, Young Adult With Issues, Friend (?), to Threat, Protocol, Something To Be Dealt With. I knew she would have to tell someone.

When I was little and I snitched on someone, my mom always used to say, 'Anthony, are you saying this to get someone into trouble or out of trouble?'

I took Sam to the hospital once. It was because she couldn't stop crying, her eyes filling up in the middle of chem class or when she thought I wasn't looking and she would pretend to search for something in her bag. She didn't need a lot of convincing. She just let me lead her like she was an old dog. I picked a hospital sort of far from the school but close to the lake because I thought: a) she wouldn't want people from the neighbourhood to be up in her business, and b) when you look at a lake sometimes you feel like that clean horizon can offer you something better than a bottle of pills.

In the emergency room we listened while the nurse in the little booth asked Sam questions. Sometimes the nurse's eyes slid over me like I was either to blame or invisible.

'What is the matter?' she said, after Sam had sighed a few times while she was punching in Sam's health card number.

'She's just … ' I said. 'I'm worried … '

'Can we let her speak, please?' said the nurse. Only she said 'please' in this impatient, bitchy way that made me feel like a bigger asshole than I already did.

'I'm just incredibly sad,' Sam said. 'In a non-negotiable way.'

The nurse looked up sharply then.

'Have you harmed yourself?' she said.

'Not today,' Sam mumbled.

And even though I'm pretty sure the nurse hadn't heard Sam, she wrote something on a form and said, 'Do you have a plan?'

Ha! It's a question we hear a lot as soon-to-be-high-school-graduates. Do you have a plan? What do you want to be when you grow up? Have you considered the pathways available to you?

Sam looked up at the nurse then and their eyes met and had a little conversation in the space between them. 'Yes,' Sam whispered.

'Okay,' said the nurse, all business again. 'A doctor will be with you soon.' She turned toward me. 'You'll stay with her?'

I nodded. Of fucking course I would.

While we were waiting, a very pregnant woman came waddling in and it was like every movie you've ever seen with a freaked-out husband carrying an overnight bag and the woman clutching at his arm and shooting him these despising looks. It made us laugh, me and Sam. Which is something normal people don't get. That you can be plotting to off yourself and still laugh at the cliché lady in labour in the ER.

Outside, the humans in uniforms are using walkie-talkies and cellphones. They are pointing at the school, making large hand movements or small nods. And behind the humans in uniform are other humans standing separately or joined, most hugging themselves. I can't see their faces exactly but I can tell by the way they are crumpled that they have been crying. And I know that I am the cause. I make my way down from my tower and find my place again between two stacks of boxes. I should not have looked. My safety, what little I had, is tainted now, and I feel myself moving further away from my body.

Why did I put the knife in my bag?

I know why. Because it is what I fear most.

On a scale of one to ten, Anthony? Her frowning, kind-eyed look. The fear is the kind of number that squeezes at your heart until your heart oozes out between fear's fingers. What is that number?

I am scared of what I want to do with the knife so I pull the knife from the bag. To face it? To hide it? To put it to use finally and rob it of its power. I roll up my sleeves. Stupid to cut across; a bit late for cries for help. I rest the tip lightly on one of the pale green veins of my wrist. And I press down.

Ant, you fuckface, what is your damage? Sam is sitting on top of my box tower and she looks good, the way she did before things got bad. I mean, still fucked up, but sort of surfing it, you know? *You're an asshole if you do this. Bleed all over this clean white paper. Traumatize all the well-adjusted folk just looking for a half-decent public school education. You need to put the knife down.*

She leans forward and squeezes her arms so that her boobs smush together in a line.

I laugh a little. Wait, what? You're trying to stop me from committing suicide by distracting me with your cleavage?

She shrugs, which just pushes her boobs up higher. *It's kinda working, right?*

It is.

You know who is the Queen of Rhetorical Questions?

I shake my head no. I know this is a new distraction technique. I turn the knife so the flat part is lying against my skin, coldly.

Sambhu's mother.

She says this like it is something I should know, or something we have discussed and debated, a shadow conversation, a BFF shorthand. But I am stumped. I shrug, but I do not let go of the knife.

You know? When she has finished telling her story?

Thus my story endeth,
The Natiya-thorn withereth.
Why, O Natiya-thorn, dost wither?
Why does thy cow on me browse?
Why, O cow, dost thou browse?
Why does thy neat-herd not tend me?
Why, O neat-herd, dost not tend the cow?
Why does thy daughter-in-law not give me rice?

Why, O daughter-in-law, dost not give rice?
Why does my child cry?
Why, O child, dost thou cry?
Why does the ant bite me?
Why, O ant, dost thou bite?
Koot! koot! koot!

Sam has relaxed her arms so that her boobs relax also. Her eyes are closed but she opens them again to repeat that last bit. Koot! Koot! Koot! She is lost: in deep memory, in dream. I have no clue what she is talking about.

Not lost, Ant. Just searching.

I put the knife down next to me. It is so heavy, and I cannot bear it with the weight of Sam's searching. The knife spins slightly on its heavy-handled axis. I place my hand on it to stop the movement. Then I pick it up and throw it across the room.

You should probably hide it somewhere.

But where? Why?

Evidence.

Evidence of what, though?

That you are a boneheaded teenage boy. There's a vent over there.

Why is Sam always so clever and correct?

ELISE

There are islands of sweet relief between contractions and I am not yet so exhausted that the outside world has begun to dissolve, although I do find myself floating free of my body, observing the organized chaos below. Thanh is snuggled in a corner – is he still sleeping? For reals? I cannot believe this can be true, not with the racket I'm causing.

I wonder if someone has thought to check his breathing. I squint through the spaces between the desks and focus on his chest as I have done many times with my son in those cavernous hours of the night – how delicate the balance between waking and sleeping, especially when the rest is so hard-won, the result of hours of jiggling and humming and silent chant-counts. To touch the baby could wake him, to creak a floorboard with my own careful weight. But not to know whether or not this small person is still here – of this world – is too much to bear.

Thanh stirs, his head jerking downward then upward. He has missed a dream-step, touched down suddenly on this earth. I wonder how he can sleep through this – not only the robust racket I am responsible for but also the weight of the situation. But I suppose we all choose our means and manner of escape.

I once had a boyfriend who would fall asleep at the first sign of stress. I used to think they were booze-induced blackouts until I started paying closer attention. It was amazing when it wasn't infuriating; he could close his eyes and deepen his breath mid-argument – and he'd be in deep, totally unreachable. Once he even did it while an amateur drug dealer, Johann, was strangling our housemate Ali in the kitchen. I learned to recognize the precursors, a shuddering yawn and a shoulder shake, then this kind of mental settling I could see in his eyes. Dead to the world on the couch while I tried my best to drag Johann from Ali's neck.

I scan the rest of the students. Strange that despite the fact that I've broken every lockdown rule with my exclamations and pacings, they are still maintaining this thin semblance of compliance, speaking in hushed, almost reverent tones, keeping low and close to the walls, out of sight. From above I notice things. A pile of old bristolboard projects wedged behind a filing cabinet. Mouse droppings in the space between the modern play cupboard and the baseboard. An empty, flattened Timbits box wedged between two dictionaries. Four VHS tapes piled on top of the corner bookshelf. I think I would like to know what those movies are and am squinting to read their cardboard sleeves when another contraction takes me, milder this time, or my body is adjusting … When I come back to my island, it occurs to me how a birth room is like the Buddhist bardo. The possibility of perfect/imperfect souls floating here, like dust motes. Or whizzing by like spitballs, ascending then nosediving like paper airplanes. Then, a chaser-thought: what a precious, bougie, middle-class, middle-aged English teacher thing to think.

There is a Christian college in the U.S. that is famous (infamous) for performing *Othello* in blackface at a time when they really should have known better. What can I say? I join in the chorus of contemporaries calling them out, dressing them down. '*Speak of me as I am. Nothing extenuate, Nor set down aught in malice.*' But how do we recognize the straitjackets we are wearing when we are mired in our own times, our own place, our own personal and cultural cosmologies? I ask myself these questions all the time, to the point where I become riddled with my own doubts, a house full of holes, drafts of history and blasts of emotion, the sighs, screams, and supremacies of humanity whistling through. And then I can't think or do anything. I'm like a less eloquent, pudgier Hamlet – with boobs. '*We must speak by the card or equivocation will undo us.*'

Maybe this is the gift of child-bearing and child-rearing; the physical urgencies drown out the natterings of the mind. I breathe my way through a contraction. I feel powerful, as though I have harnessed something. But I know the feeling will not last. Power – now, there's a tricky thing – it's not always or only conferred by position or riches. It's all about context, a word my students often have trouble with. It's the situation, I say, the place and time, the … the what's-going-on-aroundness. Like, here am I – white woman with power – thinking I can teach you, mostly non-white young people, about a play where a Black man is destroyed by a white man driven by a nascent, pernicious system of colonialism, of exploitation … But also? Jealousy. And a rotten, evil heart.

Evil.

It is parlance that is unfashionable these days, but the dude is poisoned and who knows why, really? We don't have a window into his childhood. Ha! Imagine that as an assignment! Write Iago's Student Record! It might actually work. How many times suspended? How many 46 percents bumped up to 50 percent so the weary teacher didn't have to face him glowering in the corner for another year?

What is the context now? I can imagine the students' social media posts – a quick snap of my riven, tortured form, then a catalogue of ennui. *Stuck in lockdown with my teacher who is IRL GIVING BIRTH.* I can't even. Or a story to remember? *Cool story, fam.* I find myself hoping, for their sakes as well as my own, of course my own, that the story has a happy ending. Because Dead Baby, while it might have shock value and momentary cultural currency, is not a nice thing to carry around, as anecdotes go.

The next contraction is concentrated in my lower back. It throbs and throbs, then reaches its arms around my belly, squeezing.

When it subsides, I feel intensely lucid, efficient and coherent. I think: Now for a little mental housekeeping. I hate it when they use that term in staff meetings. That and administrivia. It's the bane of English teachers everywhere, I imagine, to feel particularly irked by the means and language used to open and perpetuate the flat momentum of board of education gatherings. Here, in labour, I find myself without language, or somehow beyond it, above and beyond. Or perhaps outside of it? And it is true what they say … You forget.

I wish very much that I could remember my first labour, but there is so little I can bid back to me. There is an instinct in me to keep telling and retelling the story; to find those who bore witness and extract their accounts, to decide what has been remembered and misremembered or just subject to elision, or *finessing,* as the kids say these days. To figure out what exactly has been finessed by time. So, I rely on these eyewitness accounts, but these too seem compromised, incomplete. Because, like characters in the most page-turning of novels, we all had so much *at stake*. The midwife, goal-driven and outwardly competent; my husband, clinical and pragmatic (yet also, somehow, deeply convinced of rosy outcomes); and my own sister, yoked to me by blood and an eerie understanding of the proximity of disaster, yet miraculously calm in the midst of it. When I questioned her later, she understood my need to put the events in order, my obsession with a more omniscient point of view.

But at the time, I had no sense of differing angles, or any yearning to know visually what was transpiring at the business end of things. I was too mired in my own self, in sensations that scooped me up, God-like, then released me into new forms of being. What did it look like from the outside? Tell me. How did I scream and for how long? Where is the narrative throughline here? And when did the OB-GYN come striding in like the cavalry? Did the midwife retreat? Scuttle backward or puff up with some sense of property? I imagine the officious snap of the doctor's gloves as she pulled them on – I see the scissors gleaming like in so many emergency-room serial TV shows. And the one snip so that they could suck you out, Joey. One snip to allow for your passage into the world.

God, it hurt so fucking much.

But you forget.

Maybe.

It was all worth it.

No.

More that it was beside the point. A necessity.

It is perhaps Nate who has taught me to see it this way, although his is a different form of investment. He has little interest in building the story: a sort of end-justifies-the-means approach to narrative. And maybe he's right.

What does it matter?

Here we are.

But it does matter, doesn't it? How we got here. What it took to get us here. I try to imagine Shai-Anna having to snip the underside of my cunt. She could do it, I know. But I wonder if I could withstand or return from the searing truth of that pain again. I make a decision, like a curtain closing on a scene, that I will not consider this possibility I close my eyes, suddenly overcome with exhaustion.

Shai-Anna nudges at my knee. 'Maybe try standing or squatting, Miss. Baby's on the move.'

I nod. I am entranced by this new Shai-Anna, in her thrall. I remember a conversation we had near the beginning of the year – she had stayed behind after the bell, stacking chairs, as if it were a duty that had been foisted upon her, although I had not requested it.

Most days, she asks me, upon entering the classroom, exactly what we are doing, then weighs up her options and decides whether she will stay for the duration. Any authoritarian impulse I have is both heightened and frustrated by her behaviour. Shai-Anna is Black, Jamaican-Canadian, and has often implied I do not and cannot understand her experience. She is right. She is partially right. She is sometimes right. How do we understand each other anyway?

That day with the chairs, to fill the space and distract from her dramatic huffing, I told her about a spoken word artist I had arranged to visit the classroom to lead some workshops.

Shai-Anna continued in her task, did not look up. Ignoring me? I checked for earbuds. None. So she *had* heard.

Finally, when the chairs were all perched, the floor clear, Shai-Anna had turned toward me, suspicious. 'Is she Black?'

I hesitated. 'Half,' I said. 'Does that count?' I was being glib and confrontational, not the best means of approach; plus I hated myself for dividing a person into fractions.

Shai-Anna laughed, looked closely at me.

'You're right,' I said. 'You should have more Black teachers.' I hesitated. 'And I'm white.' I held my open palms by my side, did a semi-twirl.

Shai-Anna laughed again. 'This is an uncomfortable conversation to have, Miss.' She held my gaze, waiting for something.

'Yeah, it is. But it's okay.' I tried to stop myself from feeling a smugness, a prim sense of pride in my own humility.

'Yeah, it's okay.'

And I knew it was only partly okay, but I did not press for what I knew might be notions of justice I was not prepared to hear. I wish I had now – for righteous and completely selfish reasons – as Shai-Anna offers her arm and I hoist myself to standing, then shuffle my feet outward into a football crouch before the next contraction takes me.

CONTRACT

FADUMA

I cannot believe there is no baby yet. It seems to me something must be broken. I am moving into low-key panic mode. But Shai-Anna is still so calm. She is like a military leader in the face of terrible odds. Always strategizing. I feel something for her or toward her. What is it? Not jealousy. It is admiration. It feels like an adult word. I try it out. I admire you. But I am also worried for Miss. She looks totally exhausted in her body. This last contraction seemed to empty her out completely, her face went all loose and for a second there I know she didn't recognize me. I try to send my strength to her through my heart, where her head is now leaning, and through my hands, which she is holding on to like they are the only thing attaching her to this earth. And then I pray for her, my lips shaping the words. Inshallah.

'You must rest between contractions, Miss,' Shai-Anna says. 'Rest and breathe.'

Ryan looks lost now that the timing is kinda irrelevant. I look over at Mark, who presses his lips into a line of worry, then shrugs, then mouths something that looks like *How* or *Love* or *Help*.

I shrug back. What do I know? I turn to Ryan. 'You can wipe her head,' I say. 'Or keep it cool.'

It is something my mother does for me when I am sick – a cool hand on the forehead and a cool cloth when she has to leave my side. Ryan looks at me and nods. He pours some water from his bottle on someone's – I think Shilpa's – scarf and folds it carefully into a neat rectangular shape. Then he places it delicately on Miss's forehead.

Good, another one coming. I can feel them now like a shift in weather.

'That's it, Mumma, baby's coming,' says Shai-Anna. 'Let's keep this baby coming.'

But then Miss looks up at me and her eyes are dry and desperate and also kind of stubborn and mean.

'No,' she says. Her voice is a croak. 'I can't do it anymore. I can't.'

'You can,' I say. 'You can do this, Miss.' But Inshallah, I have never even kissed a boy, never mind lived so long so as to have another human growing inside of me and trying to make her way out into the world. I look to Shai-Anna. Has she heard? Can she cheerlead Miss through this? She meets my eyes.

SHAI-ANNA

Miss has hit a wall. When her eyes meet mine it's like she's hooked me into something and for a second I go deep into her panic and forget where my feet are planted. We know each other a little.

I stayed behind one day to help her because I wanted to throw a chair, but lifting them up above my head and setting them down again was the next best thing. Plus – I'll be real – I wanted to hang around Miss. She has this kind of buzz of concern for me all the time, even when I am obviously annoying the fuck out of her. I could tell she wanted me to talk and I considered it. But then I decided: No. Because what good would it do, really, to lay it out for this woman who couldn't possibly get what it was to listen to everybody going on and on about university applications and requirements and cut-offs and deadlines and know that it would take some kind of miracle or sugar daddy for any of that to happen for me? Still, she was lurking. Something was required of me. I slammed the last chair up on the desk. She took a few steps closer to me, which was when I saw the small swell of her belly and knew for sure what I had only suspected before. I scanned the shape of it. Four months maybe. She'd been hiding it well. But her clothes were always kind of flowy and art-teacherish, so it wasn't that hard.

'So, Shai-Anna,' she said.

I braced myself for the probing I knew was coming. So goddamn presumptuous. To believe that a person will reveal themselves just because they hang around for an extra half-hour after school. But maybe she sees something in me – my opposition – because it's not a question. It's something about a spoken word poet, and I just say it as I'm thinking it, with no delay or thought buffer: 'Is she Black?'

I've thrown her off her game but she doesn't look away. It's like we're at war but also in love.

'Half,' she says. And laughs a little. Like, in apology? Like it's her job to apologize for life.

'And you should have more Black teachers,' she says.

She says these things like they have taken something out of her. And also like she is somehow pleased with herself for saying them. So I follow the script.

'This is a weird conversation to have,' I say.

'Yes,' she says. 'But it's okay.'

I look deep into her eyes like I can maybe find something there that will help me to forgive her or help her, because somehow, without my knowing it, she has become the needy one. Which is so deeply unfair. But also: Why am I here banging chairs up on desks? I think about something she said when we first talked about English and why we study it – besides knowing how to write quarterly reports and those cheesy admissions essays in which I will have to explain exactly how *extenuating* circumstances, also known as *my life*, should qualify me for *special consideration*, also known as *financial aid*. Language is what makes us human, she said. We need our stories to make us feel human. The stories we tell ourselves. She said that they can harm or hinder us – or 'allow us the expansiveness we need to survive.'

'Yeah,' I said. But I spit it out. 'It's okay.'

ELISE

I try to throw myself forward into the moment when the baby is out, apart. As a scenario, it seems both impossible and mandatory. How will I get there?

Nate refused to cut the cord when Joey was born. He actually backed away when the midwife offered him the scissors. I could tell he saw it as an act of violence toward me, toward the baby. And I got it – it is brutal and definitive. There's a reason we use it as a metaphor for sudden and abrupt separation. To cut the cord. But still. The midwife shrugged and gave Nate a pat, then snip, right through, like it was a telephone wire. I wonder who will do it for this one or if we even have scissors sharp enough … I think there are some in the back of the desk drawer. God, they're probably filthy. I would like it to be Faduma. Shai-Anna will need to be with the baby. Hers are the capable hands, Faduma's the caring ones.

They talk a lot about love languages these days: gifts, acts of service, physical touch – there are five of them, but the last two escape me. The idea, of course, is that we cannot all proclaim it, buy roses, make grand gestures. I think Nate's love language is a loyalty to me that he only expresses to other people, when I am not there as witness. Before Joey was born, we joined a prenatal group and gamely participated in the lessons the two self-satisfied midwives led like fussy mother hens. There was one exercise – in forbearance? empathy? mindfulness? – where we were forced to hold ice cubes in our clutched hands for as long as possible. This was meant, in some twisted analogous way, to approximate the pain of childbirth, the endurance required to withstand the force of contractions as they crescendo, then crescendo again. Instead, it was a numbness concentrated in the palm that occasionally shot up to the elbow, it was water warmed by our bodies dripping slowly onto jewel-toned yoga mats.

I became pally with a wisecracking woman named Nadine, who would later confess to licking splattered vodka from the floor when the bottle fell from the freezer at 2 a.m. as she rummaged for formula to feed her perpetually colicky newborn. This was when I was still allergic to earnestness, before Joey literally split me open, trampled my heart to the point that any act of tiny magnanimity would send me into sickening choruses of *awwws*. I became a yodeller of sentiment. *Awww*. But when I met Nadine, outside the prenatal class, she was sneaking a smoke, and we both thought we could weather not only childbirth, but the whole enterprise of motherhood, with spontaneous quips and a studied irony. I thought it would be dangerous to get too *invested* in the whole thing; I didn't understand how hormones and history could hack the plan, hijack me into caring. And Nate was with me, he was, although I wonder now if he hadn't intuited something of the immensity of our shared project that I had somehow managed to elide.

At eight months along, the baby still had not turned; he remained determinedly upright, tap dancing on my bladder, his head nudging up against my lungs. When I told one of the midwife mother hens this, of the possibility of a C-section if the baby did not oblige by pointing his way out, she smiled pityingly at me.

'Oh,' she said, in a way that indicated I had failed but would be allowed to remain, swollen with child, dunce-like, within her matronly orbit, 'you can try handstands in the pool. And visualizing! Imagine that baby crowning through your vulva.' Her eyes glistened.

Nate snorted.

Rude, I thought at the time, and I meant Nate.

Later, after I had visited the pool three times, forcing my bulky body to invert itself, one hand pinching my nostrils while the other windmilled the artificial blue of the water, after I had pushed my swollen ankles up into the stuffy chlorinated air, after I had read through the thick packet of articles the midwives had gifted me – all of them decrying the C-section as somehow a betrayal of both gravity and the goddess, after I tried, I really did, to *visualize* the bowling ball of my baby's head pointing gamely toward the exit, after all of this, when the baby still had not turned, a massive sob-scream had escaped me in the middle of dinner one night. It was a dissolution that shocked Nate into embracing me as if to squeeze the last of the tears and snot out of me once and for all. When he released me I could sense his anger – what had I done? What more could I have done? Because of my lack of underwater breath control and maternal willpower, our baby would be scooped out of me like stuffing, deprived of his rightful passage. It was the beginning, it seemed to me, of a long road of missing out, the first of many opportunities I would not be able to provide him.

'I'm sorry,' I sniffed. 'He'll be *from his mother's womb untimely ripped*.' It confused me that this bit of origin story had boded so well for the good guys in *Macbeth*. I mean, I understood the loophole in the prophecy, but it seemed entirely possible the sacrifice on MacDuff's mother's part had been too steep. Sometimes I thought Shakespeare saw with the eyes of a god, sometimes the bleary, excitable gaze of a teenage boy.

But Nate was not mad at me, he was angry, furious even, with the midwives. He called them sorceresses, vinegar-tits, manipulative matriarchs. He raged for several expansive minutes on my behalf. 'What right do they have? To make you feel like you do! In the name of *what? Feminism?*'

I shrugged.

'No,' he said, 'no, no, no, no, no.'

A couple of days later, he had coaxed me out to a neighbourhood get-together. Neither of us was game, really, but it was outdoors, in a parkette-turned-outdoor rec room, concrete ping-pong tables and chessboards butting up against swing sets and slides. If a conversation turned cringe, the getaway possibilities were myriad.

I took advantage of my condition to huff and puff my way over to a log bench, lowering myself with a groan to prove my exhaustion.

From my perch, I overheard Nate describing our prenatal class to a small crowd.

'Birth and Beyond: Resisting Medicalization, Finding True Motherhood – that's what it was called,' he said. The crowd, which consisted of two women, three men, and one nonbinary person, seemed unsure how to respond.

'Well,' one of the women began.

Nate scoffed. 'They should have called it If You Get an Epidural, You're a Bee-yotch.'

God, I loved him in that moment – his scorn with my defence at its centre, his proclamation of this scorn to others but never to me. There was something cruel and noble in it. It totally turned me on.

FADUMA

'She needs energy,' Shai-Anna says. 'Water is not enough.' She scans the students in the class.

I scan with her, my eyes skipping along to the places hers have set down. I want to see what she sees. Thanh is still asleep, his legs extended out into the aisle, his body sort of accordioned down and his chin all scrunched into his chest. He looks like he could have been shot, like in a picture of one of those WWI trenches with bodies of young white men, all handsome and ... dead. Tania is doing Emily's makeup, running a big brush over her cheekbones and nose, whispering something that might be funny but I can't tell because Emily is concentrating on staying still. Kevin is trying to get with Julie, looking at her all lechy. Gross. Isaiah is staring at his phone but I don't think it's even charged. Weird. Fatou and Renata are watching a movie on Fatou's phone and Renata looks a bit pissed off, or maybe just tired. And Charlene is giving Mark a massage. WTF. None of them seems one bit interested in Miss and her tribulations. Are they really blocking it all out? Shai-Anna bumps me with her hip. I missed something. She asked me something.

'Juice,' she says. And then more loudly: 'We need juice.'

A juice box materializes and is passed down the line. Ryan peels the plastic back from the straw and pierces it through the top. I guide it to Miss's mouth and watch as she sucks it down. The difference is almost immediate. She blinks up at me, back with us again. I smile down at her but she does not smile back, taken again by the concentration required by her body.

'Okay,' says Shai-Anna. 'But it is not enough. Ryan, you need to get us Gatorade.'

Ryan shakes his head and looks over at me.

Inshallah, are those tears rising in his eyes?

'I don't want to leave her.' His voice is quiet and trembling.

'But,' I say. And I am thinking: Who will hold on to her?

And when I look up again I see in his sadness and his odd eagerness that he is volunteering for this job. So it will be me who takes on the Gatorade quest? I know suddenly – like God has done some serious convincing of my soul – that I am in fact the right person for this mission. I can feel Ryan staring at me, waiting for my decision. I can feel Miss's body resting against my chest. I can feel first her breathing and then her body's massive tensing. And I know it is up to me to go out there and bring her back the sustenance she needs to do this crazy awesome thing. Maybe the most important job in the universe.

'Okay,' I say to Ryan. 'I'll go.'

Ryan looks both relieved and terrified.

I place my hand on Miss's face, so she looks up at me. 'I need to get you some Gatorade,' I say, staring deep into her eyes so the message reaches her brain. 'Don't worry, Ryan will stay with you.' She looks confused and abandoned – like a puppy – and for a second I doubt my decision. But then Ryan speaks up.

'It's okay, Miss.' He is beside me, looking down into the bowl of her face. 'I'm here.'

He nudges me out of the way, and in the pause between contractions we manage the transfer. He is holding her now, his arms snaking down her sides to clutch at her hands.

'Don't squeeze too hard,' I say. 'And you have to breathe with her.'

He nods, but I can tell he is already all in with this new duty. He will do a good job. Shai-Anna looks up at me.

'Basement machine, next to the small gym,' she says. 'You got change?'

Fuck. I shake my head.

But it is as if the world, which is our classroom, has heard and suddenly all these kids have their hands out – the opposite of begging – offering me whatever it is they have scrounged from the bottom of their pockets, backpacks, pencil cases, fake Gucci purses.

I collect the coins, then look back over to Shai-Anna, who meets my eye in this stern, respectful way. Like we are comrades, equals. Is it wrong that it makes my heart swell a little? I collect the money quickly, put all the coins in the pockets of my abaya. There's no point counting it now. I'll just feed it into the machine and hope for the best when I make it there. If I make it there. Inshallah. *When* I make it there.

I shake out my legs, which are stiff from acting like Miss's easy chair. One of my feet has pins and needles. I stumble a bit and Shai-Anna reaches out to steady me.

'You good?' she says, but doesn't look up at me.

'I got this,' I say, which feels stupid, because I'm pretty sure I don't.

When I get to the classroom door, Mark looks at me like I am crazy and blessed. Which I guess I am. Which I know I am. I feel my face get hot and then I'm ashamed. How can I be thinking about a crush when there is a baby trying so hard to be born?

'Good luck,' he says, looking right into my eyes so that something slides like liquid honey down the back of my neck to the base of my spine. 'You ready?'

I nod. I am ready.

He turns the doorknob and pulls the door open.

'Live long and prosper,' I say, before I can stop myself. OMG.

Then the door closes behind me and that's it. I'm out. Locked out and locked down.

It seems right to me that I leave the high ceilings of the main floor for the basement as soon as possible. I shuffle-run to the staircase. I want so badly to feel enclosed again. I want to take cover. I take the stairs quickly, listening to the rasp of my own breath.

But by the time I get to the bottom, my steps feel nimble. I can feel something happening inside my body. A kind of oiling of the machine. It is Allah giving me this strength, this courage. Thank you, I whisper, over and over, under my breath. I understand myself now to be on a quest. I have left all that is familiar, my community, my townsfolk, and made my way down to the underworld, the dark woods, the unknown. To boldly go ... What obstacles will I face? I can see the diagram Miss drew when we looked at the monomyth at the beginning of the year, the circular journey I am on ... Shit. I didn't bring anything to carry the bottles back in. I will have to use my abaya as a bag.

The monomyth – or the hero's quest – it was Joseph Campbell who came up with it, or named it, I guess, because his whole point was that it's been around forever, just kind of lurking inside our human hearts throughout history. It's the idea that stories, across culture and geography and time, all stories share this kind of pattern where the hero's world is somehow thrown off balance and he has to leave or is exiled and has to find the key or the treasure so that he can return home and restore harmony. It's cool how it can be applied to *Star Wars*, and Hansel and Gretel, and also the Buddha. I told my dad about it one day on the way home in the car. He listened but didn't say much. Then, as we were pulling into the driveway, he said, 'Faduma, child, no one ever leaves home unless their home is unsafe, quest or no quest. Go inside. Your mother may need you.'

I have reached the pop machine. It stands before me like an oasis in a desert, looming and large, like it is a whole building, a whole world I must enter if I want to succeed. The first coin I insert, a loonie, comes boomeranging back through the machine's workings and falls uselessly into the return slot. I retrieve it and hold it up to my mouth, breathe on it like I've seen gamblers do with dice on TV shows. Then I insert it again, gently, so gently, and listen closely to its progress. I can tell it has hit its destination and will not return. Success! The two quarters follow smoothly, and the red numbers on the small black screen next to the slot show I have reached my goal. I watch for the withdrawal of the barrier that holds the bottles back. The wait is agonizing.

The *thunk* of the bottle falling is so loud and final. And dangerous! This noisy evidence of me, roaming outside of my home, which is my classroom, away from my people, my classmates. I push my hand past the trap door and work the bottle free. It is heavy in my hand, bright with its unnatural red contents.

I am working the second bottle free of the machine when something happens inside my chest. It's like Allah was inside me, animating me, and then He just left with a *whoosh* through my heart, and my heart is speeding up, chasing Him with its beats. And I know, I do, that Allah is always with me. But I cannot sense Him. And I can't get a proper breath. It's like the air stops in my throat and can't make it down to my lungs. Will prayer let me find Him again? And what right do I have to call on Him? He is busy I know but He is everywhere and I need Him. My chest tightens.

I allow my brain to travel, as if on a high-speed train, to the place where I do not leave, where I do not make it out of the classroom, out of the school, where I am instead stuck in this moment, with these people, and it all ends. My mind goes to my mother. I watch her collapse and keen. I hear her ululations and gasps, her mouth wide open to the Heavens, grieving in a way I have seen only once before, when the news came about her sister, left behind in the camp, taken by tuberculosis. And my father? His grief would be quieter; there would be a lot of prayer and a clutching of the face, the gut. He would use his hands to hold himself together.

Fuck that.

I cannot die in front of the pop machine. I have a job to do. And it would be so undignified. Would Mark be sad? The thought comes without my permission. Wrong thought. Haram central. No wonder Allah left me. Will Miss's baby die if she doesn't get this sustenance? The thought makes my heart beat faster; it is beating up into my throat now. My heart is trying to escape my body. And my breath is not doing its job. I try to pray. I imagine I am my father praying. And I try to imagine what my father might do. I am already on my knees, my hand stuck in the pop machine. I bring my forehead down to the floor in supplication. And I hear my father's voice, stern and clear. *Faduma. Daughter. Knowledge is the light that overcomes evil.* What the fuck. Not helpful when your hand is in the guts of a pop machine and a pregnant lady is counting on you. It makes me laugh. And when I laugh, I relax a bit, which allows Allah to slip back in through my nostrils and bring me some small peace. Of course Allah is there. He never left you, says my father. I think of my father in the Kenyan camp, playing soccer in the dirt, protecting his mother from the man who broke through their fence, held a knife to her throat, stole what little they had. It should not be so hard for me to be brave. The bottle falls and I wiggle it free. I can get more; I will get more.

ELISE

Elise thinks she might die. The realization comes to her in a soft wave between contractions. It is not alarming as realizations go. It has the mereness of truth about it. There are eventualities, and death is one of them. Hers will not be a hero's death. She has not sprung to action or devised a clever means of escape, rigged up makeshift tools for sustenance or comfort. No, she has conscripted the very children in her charge as helpmates, as servants to her own biological drive for survival. She is selfish. So be it. But to die now? It is so unsatisfying. Where is the threat they have barricaded themselves against? Never mind. She is tired. It would be okay to die, *to sleep, perchance to dream, for in that sleep of death what dreams may come?* Not dreams in this purgatorial space but memories, memories with the heft and shape of dream, suppressed or half-remembered. Her faithfulness to Nate fashioned and sustained through her own wistful, wishful thinking.

She had left that conference table full of colleagues drunk on both mediocre red and the sublime power of Shakespeare's enduring texts – still – in this age of handheld computers and chemotherapy. Hers was a different intoxication, the kind of desire she knew was chemical, pheromonal, animal – and was no less possessed by it for knowing its provenance. She had half stumbled, half run into the small patch of woods that adjoined her B and B.

Of course he found her.

She was broadcasting her want like an emergency beacon. She was shouting out to him in cunt-talk. She knew what happened in the woods – site of transformation, of fairy tale magic and horror. What happens in the woods stays in the woods. And it had until now. She does not remember vibrating with yearning, scrambling over boulders, stumbling off the wood-chipped path, conjuring him like she had the birds, the cicadas buzzing, her brain buzzing, the overwhelm of woods and body, how desperately she wanted him to appear and then he did, disturbing small slow creatures, kicking at loose patches of moss and assemblages of twigs with his near-pristine hiking boots. What strange lenses lust fashions for us. *Love looks not with the eyes, but with the mind, And therefore is winged Cupid painted blind.* She knew she had never met anyone as beautiful, as consumable, as fine. He kissed her up against a tree, the bark pressing into her bra strap a happy annoyance. Her hands found his butt, made a basket for it, drew it close. And then his mouth was the small slow creature, on her neck, on her breast – too unbearably, wonderfully slow, then so very still (but trembling) as they breathed into what they were making. And he was inside of her, moving. And then the smells of them, the smells of the loam and pine needles. The scud of the clouds overhead. A shivering that set the world to rights.

So. Elise is dying in childbirth and can't stop thinking about how she boned a guy amidst a patch of pine trees outside a small-town B and B eight years ago. So it goes. Forgive me, Nate. Forgive me, small one, still struggling for life.

Words fly up / Thoughts remain below / words without thoughts / Never to heaven go

She feels a grip on her shoulder. Nate? No, Ryan, his gaze trained on Elise's slack countenance. Come back, Miss, he is saying. We are here. You can do this.

But Elise doesn't want to leave the woods for this box that smells of her beleaguered body's striving, teenage sweat, chalk dust, industrial cleaners, and the perfumed ghosts of the colonial canon. She wants to stay in the woods, where she is powerful, where she is fucking, where she is free.

SHAI-ANNA

I can see how Miss is fading and the baby is stalled. There are no instruments here to measure its tiny heartbeats, no professionals to call on for help, for rescue. It is me, and me only, who will bring this new life into the world. And I am all of a sudden furious. There are so many things in my life I never asked for, why the fuck should I add this to the list? I try to pray, but my relationship to God is held together by a shitty modem, the kind most people still have on little islands with no money. Still, that's the last place I think I might have seen Him, or It, or Them, I guess, if I'm being gender-inclusive. Even though it felt like we were in Butt-fuck, Nowhere, when I saw those puppies slide out of their mumma, I did believe in God or maybe I just thought I was capable of believing. It makes me dizzy to think about it.

The puppies looked like stretched-out amoebas, not even creatures yet. They were slick and whitish, like they'd crawled out of a cloud instead of a wet, bloody womb, and for a second they just lay there, barely whimpering.

'Are they dead?' I asked my granmumma.

'Nuh-uh, child, they just decidin' some things.'

What were they deciding? I didn't ask. It seemed this was something I was expected to know. The mother dog roused herself again and walked in a small, then smaller, circle. She kept scuffing and scooping at the earth.

'She's makin' dem all a home.'

And I remember thinking that was all it took to make a home. A small circle and some scooping out of space to make things comfy, your own. And that was when I thought maybe that mumma dog and her puppies or maybe God or maybe Granmumma – someone was trying to teach me a lesson.

Later, when I was older, and sometimes thought of myself as wiser, I would remind myself of this – when the apartment's balcony seemed to be teasing me with its tininess, when I heard my classmates talk about vacations or cottages on lakes with docks that ended in blue sky and blue water. A home can be made. It can be magicked. And I remembered Adio and Bob, the green light of that forest fort, the light of Adio's admiration.

Those puppies being born showed me something of childbirth, but just a tiny fraction. Female humans – bipeds – make a much larger racket bringing babies into this world. I can't say it prepared me. No, it didn't prepare me. Maybe it just primed me to want to witness it; it made me curious. But curious is not the same as wanting to *help your teacher give birth during a motherfucking lockdown*. God? A little assist might be good right about now. I know you got wars and famines and general chaos to oversee, but hello? I'm seventeen.

I look over at Faduma, who has returned with an army's worth of Gatorade. Ridiculous. And also: Who needs God when you have people like her?

'I got you,' she mouths, but looks really shy saying it.

ENG4U1-03

We are beyond restless now, an energy beating through us, sizzling through our limbs. How long now? Three hours, twelve minutes, forty-six seconds. There is a world outside: chaos and danger. In here there is safety, however provisional, short-lived. We clutch our phones like they will help us, like they might help her, but we are aware of Shai-Anna's edict, and some of us are crying but trying not to show it and some of us are bawling into our own sleeves or the shoulders of our friends because now there is no plan, there is just a racket. It's like raccoons fighting or fucking – no, it's like crack-heads scrambling for a fix – no, it's like angry hippos talking trash. Who put Shai in charge anyway? You think you could do better? Where the fuck are the police? Why we always runnin' from the police and now you in love with them? Uh, yeah, because this is beyond CRAY. Does anyone have any food? Can't she just shut up? What's the first thing you gonna do once you outta here?

FADUMA

There is something wrong. We are losing her. To what?

'What is wrong?' I ask Shai-Anna, who shakes her head grimly.

Inshallah. Bring her back, bring her back.

ELISE

Things could have been different for her; it is true, she admits now, that she had wanted them to be different. But how different, really, would they have been? She had waited for Devin in a small vestibule outside the conference room on the final day. It seemed obvious to her that he would pass through, that their encounter was somehow destined. But whatever cosmic pool cue had sent them clacking against each other in the woods was not in play that day. She waited, leaning up against an oatmeal-coloured wall, a poor, posture-addled approximation of that ardent moment pressed into the tree. The fluorescent lights buzzed overhead, then flickered. There was a single chair in the corner, dark brown vinyl, shiny chrome tubing. But she refused to sit. It would mean defeat, wouldn't it? Or something else, some lack of nonchalance, some acknowledgement that what happened had been important, a transgression, an opening to an otherworldly possibility. Or worse: a giving in, a surrender to the notion that what they had was unremarkable, a fumbling in the forest that could only lead to disappointment, to the dull day-to-day. She wanted transcendence. You didn't sit in a vinyl chair to wait on transcendence. (But he never came.) In this way her fate was decided. *Our thoughts are ours / Their ends none of our own.*

SHAI-ANNA

No. No, no, no, no, no. Nonononononono.

I will not let you go. Come now, woman. Come back.

ELISE

What floats into my mind's eye? An image of my grandmother on her deathbed, genderless and pale, in the moments after she stopped breathing. She was like a statue, noble and dense, her nose, which had become bulbous and rosy in life, now patrician and porcelain-like. Where did she go? It does not do to dwell on these questions for too long at the moment of a loved one's passing. I save them for discussions of literature – the safety of the classroom. Hamlet's interminable ruminations, the undiscovered country from whose bourn no traveller returns – he'd be prescribed past those soliloquies now, wouldn't he? Or speak them haltingly to a professional trained to curtail the lushness of his doomsaying.

My own mother has this look of not death exactly but past death – I see it sometimes when she falls asleep in front of the ten o'clock news, a purr of a snore rising from her. The engine of life still very much in order but some absence of self at play. It frightens me to my core, but I force myself to watch for a moment, to be with her while she has flown away. I wonder if Nate has seen this in me? This is why I must ask for their stories – the ones who saw me do this incredible thing. And now? A whole room full of onlookers watching me leave myself, watching my body buck and heave.

I open my eyes to Shai-Anna's brown ones staring down at me, and I realize she is scared. I have traumatized her. I begin to laugh, to chuckle – ugh, it is a word I hate! – with the notion of the journal reflections I will assign my students upon my return. *Describe the atmosphere in the classroom while Ms. Foster was giving birth.* The hubris! To bring another human into this world. To ask another human to witness and record their impressions of me and my workings as I do so.

ANTHONY

It is possible I fall asleep for a minute or an hour, because when I open my eyes again, Sam is sitting on the same stack of paper, but she looks bored, almost impatient.

Inpatient, she says, smiling. *I'm your own personal inpatient, Ant. What's happening outside?*

I climb back up my makeshift ladder to check. The scene out the window has shifted, appears more regulated, militarized almost. Where before there was chaos and worry and a kind of amped-up waiting floating around, now it seems there is a mission, that there are people, men, in charge. All of the parents are roped off behind a yellow plastic police ribbon.

Huh. I've always found that police tape so weird. It looks so flimsy and festive. Happy.

Easy for you to say. I am getting angry with Sam. She is so casual and opinionated for someone so formless.

Not really, she says. *Not that easy.*

Sorry, I say, but more to end the conversation than to make amends. I love her so much my intestines have twisted up with it but suddenly I understand that I can't be alone anymore.

You're not alone.

I need a crowd. Bodies and body odour. Stupid pushing up against puberty. And – despite myself – I really want to see Maria.

When I look out the window again, I see that the uniforms have crept like spiders to the edges of the building, looking for a way in. And I know I have to go back to room 108.

SHAI-ANNA

The last time I saw my granmumma she took me aside, then out the back door of her ramshackle house and sat me down on an upside-down mango crate. Then she walked in circles around me as she spoke, her wide hips rocking back and forth as she shifted from one foot to another. The air was thick with rain to come and my sinuses were feeling it, like some pissed-off weather duppy was squatting there.

'You should sit, Granmumma,' I said. 'Rest your bones.'

She shook her head no even though I could see sweat starting to bead on her forehead. 'I'm not dead, just old. Best keep moving. Best tell my story standing up.'

I closed my eyes and pinched at the pain at the bridge of my nose.

'Cowrie shells,' she began. 'Common enough but can reproduce like dollar bills made of flimsy paper or shiny plastic. Now, the trading that's bad, never that, no, it's dem boys who chase the green devil with her drugs and pistols. What yuh say? But! To trade a shell that was once a sea snail's home. A beautiful shiny yeye, an opening, a punny, the entryway to a soul or to a womb! In that, their meaning, they're sacred.'

I had opened my eyes but was not looking at her. I didn't like that she had used the word *punny*. A bird squawked. A moped squawked in reply. There were shouts in the distance, kids calling to each other as they raced down a dirt road, and the smell of allspice and trash fires.

'When yuh grow, Shai, promise me this, yes? That yuh understand what it means to be rich.'

I nodded. The rocking of her hips was hypnotic. Her circling like a song that kept its time through something old and creaking and tangled in roots. I felt stupid thinking these things. She was a foolish old lady and I was a girl with too little to lose.

'There are many, many varieties, but this one? Rare.' She pulled a shell from the pocket of her housedress and pinched it between two fingers, holding it up to show me. She was going to give it to me and I didn't want her to. The moment felt too big. I caught myself before the kiss reached my teeth. She was old and did not deserve my disrespect. She let the shell, which was the size of a nickel, tumble into her palm. It was the colour of bone, brown freckles along its slash of a mouth, networked with imperfect lines on its back.

'It's rare, this one, Shai-Anna.' She kept walking but turned her head to keep her eyes on me as she circled. 'For fertility we wear dem as belts round our middles, close to where the baby's housed. But yuh, yuh I think should wear it round yuh neck close to yuh mind cuz they're things waiting to be born there and yuh will need to protect them mind-babies yuh grow.'

I nodded. I had a chain at home, sterling silver, mid-length. I could feel the shell already, at the base of my throat, where my heartbeat lived.

'To strengthen the thoughts, that strong will that yuh harnessing.' She passed the shell to me.

On the next circle she turned and rock-stepped back into the house. Like she had just finished feeding the chickens or hanging out the washing. And left me sat there. Holding a seashell like it was gold.

I know who needs the cowrie shell now.

'Faduma,' I say. 'Can you undo this?' I point to my neck.

Faduma looks confused. She always looks confused. Confused or loving? It is irritating.

'Oh, is it in your way?' She asks this like a dental assistant.

'No, I just need it ... She needs it.' My confidence leaves me. I hear my mother's voice. Nonsense and superstition. Spells and amulets! I muster some anger and launch it toward Faduma. 'Take it off.' Then I feel her hands at the nape of my neck, gentle and efficient, as though she knows what all of this means, and I feel sorry for a second.

'Here,' she says, and hands me the shell. 'It's beautiful.'

FADUMA

I unclasp the necklace carefully – was it choking her? The charm is a small off-white shell with a mouth-like opening running its length. It has a pearly sheen to it. Pretty, I guess. I pass it to her. She does not meet my eye so I return to my post at Miss's head. Miss's exhaustion has possessed her entirely now. Her eyeballs have rolled back, but the lids flutter when I tell her it's okay, that it's all going to be okay. The skin on her face is flushed and dull. I am struck by an obvious fact: my mother did this same thing to bring me here, into this world. And then my father saved me from this same world. And now? They want love and success for me. A job and a wedding, and maybe children of my own. My father wants to stand up in the mosque and declare my place, my belonging in the order of things. He would like to invite them all to celebrate my marriage!

But I want a small wedding, I have told him. I have imagined the glisten of gold embroidery on my dress, the clink of gold bangles on my wrists, my groom's face still a sweet blur, unknowable.

'Bah,' my father says. 'If the guests do not fit, they will stand in the parking lot. But we must invite them!'

'But I don't know them!'

'Still,' says my father, 'the parking-lot people are important.'

I know what Miss might say: male privilege, the patriarchy, the tyranny and trap of marriage, of tradition. And she is right. But sometimes I think there are things she does not know. Like our kind of love. Like what it means to feel held by your people and your God.

Shai-Anna is whispering something in Miss's ear, an incantation or instruction or scold. I watch her take the shell from her necklace and place it in Miss's hand, wrap her own hand around Miss's closed one, give it a pat that looks like blessing.

Shai-Anna meets my eye. 'Now,' she says. 'Hold on to her. We need to get this baby.'

ELISE

'Miss? Miss? I know you will want to push. Do not push. Baby's not quite ready to be born.'

How does she know these things? In the cell of time between contractions, I see my husband hovering near the desk. Oh, thank god, he has arrived. He is smiling beatifically and holding himself perfectly still. What the fuck? Does he think calm observation does any good in these situations?

We had argued. Not this morning, but a few mornings ago. And I took seriously the maxim of never leaving the house angry. Going to bed angry didn't bother me so much – the person would still be there, maddening and intractable, in the morning. But if he left the house carrying a festering hurt or gnawing fury? Who knew what he might encounter on the outside, where dangers and temptations lived. It is perhaps true of all long-marrieds that the very things that seemed electric and new, that held immense, undeniable appeal about their partner in the beginning, become somehow anathema as time wears on, as circumstances and hormones and the vagaries of personality shape and reshape us.

Nate's steady sense of control, his unflappability, the slight, loving way he mocked my own anxiety and tendency toward relentless feeling, the comfort of all this oppositeness, his primness and strength to my (relative) wantonness ... How I loved and craved all of it! To me he seemed so zen and tranquil, a pool whose ripples barely registered on its surface. A great balm to all that was plaguing me. I liked that he discounted my feelings, reined them in. That he still insisted on setting an alarm on weekends; that I could tease him sometimes into relaxing his vigilance. And now? There are moments I want nothing more than to cannonball into that zen pool, to crash headlong into his counterfeit calm, even though I understand its purpose for him as scaffolding to the self – and for us: one half of the definition that has constrained and carried us through the years.

We fought over my decision to buy a new crib for the baby. I found it online of course, through a slick mummy blog I would have scoffed at mere weeks ago – but there is something to this nesting thing; I feel it in my immense longing for shiny, soft things, and for the things that might, if we are lucky, protect us from the slings and arrows of outrageous fortune. The crib was solid wood, Scandinavian in design; it promised a life of clear purpose. It was astronomically expensive. We could not afford it. When I showed it to Nate, he blinked slowly, then laughed a bark of a laugh. And I hated him for not even entertaining the prospect of such useful, extravagant beauty. Later that night, much later, when I woke to shooting pain in my hips, a dry mouth, and swirling thoughts, I knew with calm certainty that the crib was the answer. I ran my fingers over the numbers on my credit card as if reading a magical form of Braille, then typed those same numbers into the designated window with conviction. It was done. It was such an aggressive satisfaction I felt. I decided not to tell Nate until the day it was to be delivered. I returned to bed, wedged the body pillow under my bulk, and slept soundly until dawn. But in the morning, when Nate frowned at the cereal bowl I had left in the sink, some swollen flakes floating like lily pads in a puddle of milk, I couldn't help myself. I blurted it out.

'I bought the crib,' I said.

Nate just sighed and grabbed at both elbows, a gesture I recognized as a sign of irritation and a form of self-soothing.

'We'll talk about it later,' he replied.

Later? As if I were a recalcitrant child. Rage bubbled up in me. 'No, we fucking won't. I bought the crib because I *want* the crib.'

He had backed out the door, hands raised in mock surrender, keys and phone clutched in one of them. As if he were escaping.

I try to wave at him, but Faduma is squeezing my hand much too hard, and when I try to tell her as much, another contraction rocks me, and when I look up again, Nate is gone, evaporated.

ENG4U1-03

We really, like really, need to pee. Some of us need to actually shit. Like to evacuate our bowels. Because this has dragged on long enough that our guts know what maybe our brains don't. Something is wrong. Why haven't they saved us? Or released us at least. Three hours, thirty-three minutes. We feel abandoned and examined. Both. A petri dish of goat-scented sweat, austerity measures, baked-in racism, drab colonial decor – I'm looking at you, Queen Elizabeth. And now? Diarrhea, motherfuckers. What we would like is just to have some peace, some privacy, a space free of clueless overseers, the homophobic home boys, the meanest of mean girls. A place to poo. A bathroom of one's own.

MARIA

Over the following weeks, Lucy wrote to me: long, confessional emails of the sort I used to type in a frenzy to my first true love, when email was still new – those letter/diary hybrids we loved so much because they zoomed off to the recipient just like that. In her notes to me, which began without intro or greeting, she would speak/write as though sitting across from me at a café or sunk in a friend's couch. She spoke to me as though I were her sister, and she was the sister I never had – and I suppose this intimacy, which seemed different from the intimacy I shared with many of my clients, hooked me in. She spoke to me as if she knew me and as if this knowledge, rather than my willingness to listen, was what allowed her to open up to – as the kids would say – spill the tea.

I will never leave him. Lord knows I've tried. A whole narrative has played out for me – and it's not just Anthony holding me here. I know the line: we stayed together for the child. But it has never been only that, although that's part of it, of course it is. Do I think he'd have been better off if we'd split? Sometimes I think so. I know what he saw and what it looked like. I would never have done it. I just wanted Ian to feel the fear, the frustration, that I feel. I don't think I would have done it; my sense of consequence is still too acute. We'd had too much to drink. Not an excuse. Just a fact, part of the picture, you know? It's not a thing, really, women killing their partners, their kids. More of an aberration. Even to take off on them. Still strange, taboo. To build a nest, feather it, then just soar off into the clouds. I know that to be bound to a person has its sweet freedoms as much as it chafes at the soul. But the feeling of being yoked to him sometimes. It chokes me.

I understood from the outset that I should have shut it down, refused her access to my electronic self, and there were times I tried, I really did. My polite refusals are still sitting in my drafts folder, waiting. But I will never send them. I wanted her to need me; I craved it. And, here is the shameful part, considering what I knew about Anthony. I wanted to live inside her story, for her to continue trusting me, unburdening herself to me. I had always known I would not have children, and her story both vindicated and taunted me. To never be capable of giving myself over the way she did, to the volatility of her heart. And to know that this decision to remain apart and hungry was probably the best one for me. The way she described her bond with Anthony – a shared source or secret. I was on the outside looking in – a position I normally enjoyed for the protection and insight it offered me, but in this case found discomfiting and strange.

When Anthony was eleven we went on vacation to PEI, *just for a week in the summer. We don't often have a lot of extra cash for these types of breaks but somehow it felt less frivolous because it was domestic, because what could even go wrong in a place that felt like a drawing on a postcard? It was that unreal and ideal. We drove because it was cheaper – and for the adventure! But halfway there, Ian had a heart attack while driving. Or at least we thought it was a heart attack. And Ant and I had to sit there on the verge – one of the saddest places in the whole world, the edge of a highway – waiting for the ambulance while Ian sat in the car, slumped against the steering wheel, refusing or unable to speak to us, focusing instead on the pain, on staving off the pain, and also the end of the pain, which we were sure would mean he was a goner. Would mean nothingness. Anthony was quiet too. He picked long blades of grass and braided them together, then tore delicate pieces of skin from the edges of his fingernails. When the paramedics arrived, he hugged one of them when she climbed out of the ambulance, and didn't seem to care when she pushed him away.*

I thought of Anthony then, and the many ways we find to betray each other, mostly without meaning to. I thought of how love morphs, with misunderstanding, with misfiring, into anger. And I thought of my solo self with tenderness, with blessing.

I think it would have been easier if it was a heart attack instead of a panic attack. It might have fused us together somehow. It is still too difficult to believe that a person can experience that much pain and numbness from a kind of amped-up worry. I drove the rest of the way. We listened to a lot of bad talk radio and easy-listening jazz. Anthony sometimes sketched in the back seat or scanned Instagram when the reception wasn't spotty. We ate a lot of pickle chips and drank root beer. Anthony was the best at burping on demand. And when we got there? I just didn't know how to speak to Ian anymore. And all he could seem to do was smile weakly and smoke pot once Anthony had gone to bed. I still loved him – I just didn't know what to do with him.

ELISE

Shai-Anna's eyelashes are lovely. I love them. I love her, her assertive beauty and amazing, surprising competence. Not surprising, no, just arresting – in these circumstances – to understand that I have mischaracterized her, or misidentified her strengths. I will have to call her mother.

SHAI-ANNA

Miss is looking at me all gooey-eyed. I worry that the pain has unhinged her, or that there are disasters afoot I can't see or prevent.

I know what could happen because I saw it with my auntie's third baby. My mumma had called the midwife despite my auntie saying, 'No, I'm fine, just a bit of indigestion.'

But my mumma knew the signs, she could see from Beatrice's face and I could too, the way her eyebrows came down like awnings over her eyes and for a moment it was like she was concentrating on reading a book nobody else could see – and then she was free of it.

'Maybe,' she said to my mother, 'but don't fret, they is far apart.'

'Gyal,' said my mother, who had a way of telling time that needed no watch. 'They is five minutes apart.' She handed her the phone. 'Call,' she said. 'And don't give me no lip.' I knew to pay attention; my mother was using patois.

Then Beatrice looked at my mother with her hands on her hips and a new one came – the eyebrows, the invisible book – and when she came back she nodded and took the phone.

'Denial,' my mother whispered to me. 'Not just a river in Egypt.' It was one of her only jokes, and she used it so often it was less like a joke and more like a kind of song, a repeated riff we shared that meant more or less depending on the situation. Sometimes when she said it, it made no sense at all; she muttered it to the TV or in the middle of a grocery aisle. Other times she used it as a scold – if she thought I was slacking off or playing when I should be working. Not just a river in Egypt.

The midwife was Iranian and I loved the look of her face even though she scared me a little – maybe because I could tell my mother respected her and to prompt my mother's respect was no small thing. Shirin had the clearest, most lovely olive skin. It looked so unbelievably smooth on her chubby arms when she pushed up her sleeves. Somehow, in combination with her way, which was bossy as fuck, the clean plumpness of her arms and the way her deep brown eyes looked directly into mine made me believe she knew her shit. Beatrice's bedroom was already set up; the clean sheets stacked, the bed piled with firm pillows, the crucifix staring down at us from the wall above the bed. Beatrice squatted and grunted through a round of contractions and then tore off her clothes like they were on fire. Like she was on fire.

'You have to lie down now,' Shirin said softly. 'I need to check your cervix.'

'Fuck off,' Beatrice said. Calmly and so clearly.

'Egypt,' muttered my mumma, waiting to see what would happen next.

Shirin was so still and soft. But I knew she was strong too.

'Beatrice.' Shirin laid her hand on my auntie's shoulder and Beatrice shook it off. 'You must lie down on the bed.' She cut her eyes toward Jesus. Just a quick flick, but Beatrice saw.

'Byeeotch,' Beatrice said. But she moved her bulk over to the bed. Slowly, she lowered herself down, her bottom spread wide. My mumma was there, her arms open to hold on to her sister from behind, to allow Beatrice to lay her head against her breast.

Shirin inserted her gloved hand into my auntie and nodded. 'You can push soon.'

When it was time for Beatrice to push, Shirin turned to me. 'Hold her hand, Shai-Anna. Make sure the heart monitor stays in place.' She pointed to the small machine strapped like a seat belt around Beatrice's belly. I did as I was told.

'I can see baby's head,' said Shirin. 'But you must stop pushing.'

'The cord,' Mumma whispered to me, when I looked to her for answers. 'The cord is tangled.'

I will not have time to prepare, will not have Shirin's soft stillness, if Miss's baby is, as they say, in distress. Such polite-sounding words for being choked by a rope that used to bring you food.

What did I realize at that moment when the baby was stuck, the heart monitor beeping like some mad thing? I realized that things could be settled one way or another in those bottomless minutes. I had never really understood the idea of 'a matter of life and death.' It is a cliché, as Miss would say. But people use clichés because they are *true*. We just let them flow over or whiz by us because we've heard or read them so many times. But they're like stop signs or traffic signals on the way home. Just because we don't notice them anymore doesn't mean they aren't important.

Shirin was not shaken, but I could see even my boulder rock of a mumma begin to tremble a bit at her edges. And my auntie? She looked like maybe her angels and her devils were having it out inside of her. I saw her eyes roll back in her head and then a look of terrifying peace came over her. Like she had surrendered when the last thing we needed was for her to give up.

And then – it was so strange – even though I could see right through to the absolute worst, to Dead Baby, I felt a quiet in my core, like I could survive this and I would not be the one losing my shit. It was clarity. Something I never feel in my daily life. I looked at Shirin and I could tell she felt it too, that I could partner her in this more than my own mumma. We're gonna live by our sharpened wits, I felt like saying to her. And we're gonna make this happen. But that was for a second only, the time it took for the heart monitor to chatter away, telling its own story.

'Shai-Anna,' Shirin said. 'You come here.' She beckoned me down toward Beatrice's knees. I flanked my auntie like an attendant to some royal. And it's true, a woman giving birth is never more like a queen. A rude and roaring queen. A formidable queen.

And Shirin said, 'Beatrice, your baby is in trouble and I need you to be brave. This will hurt.'

I was surprised to hear Shirin address the pain of childbirth; it did not seem her way to discuss hardship.

Beatrice whimpered and I watched my mumma wipe sweat from her sister's brow.

'Hold her knees steady,' Shirin told me. Then she looked up to meet Beatrice's eyes again. 'You must not push, Beatrice. It's coming, I can feel it, but you must hold off while I sort things out. Do you understand?'

My auntie's eyes were wild so my mumma nodded for her. When the contraction came, my aunt howled to the heavens. Shirin reached her hand inside, then shook her head.

'We have to get the baby out before I can untangle it.'

We. Even in the eye of that emergency I noticed that word and hung on to it.

'Next time you can push, Beatrice, but gently, gently. Do you understand?'

I thought there was no way that Beatrice could hear what Shirin was saying. She was too far gone. But she nodded, eyes closed, and a *yes* escaped her lips like a curse. Mumma got her to pant, little puffs of breath, when the next one came. I watched Shirin guide that tiny skull into its new world, then slip her fingers under the cord that was wrapped twice around the neck and ease it just a little so that when Beatrice pushed the next time, the cord was looped like a fancy choker and Shirin could slip it carefully, carefully over the baby's neck.

My aunt was barely conscious when we laid her babe on her breast. Mumma stayed with them until they both slept. I helped Shirin tidy up, and before she left she clasped me to her like a comrade.

'That was good work, Shai-Anna,' she said. 'The best kind of work.'

My Mumma let me stay home from school the next day even though I had no fever or vomiting. I stayed in bed until afternoon and I slept like the dead. There was a heaviness to my body I didn't think possible. I could barely lift my head from the pillow at 2 p.m. and it wasn't until four-thirty that I dragged myself into the kitchen. Mumma had made stew.

'Sustenance,' she said to me.
'Not hungry,' I said, wiping the crust from the corners of my eyes.
'Egypt,' she replied, and ladled me up a bowl.

PUSH

MARK

Mark hears a knocking at the door, almost lost in the sounds Miss is making, deep bellows and short gasps – surrender and resistance and … love? Yes, he thinks, all of these. And simple pain too, a pain that splits the air. He imagines at first that this other noise is in his head, because he has pictured it so forcefully, what will happen when the intruder finally finds them, what will happen when the rescuers finally breach their sanctum, discover and save them. He stops, tries to separate Miss's cries and Shai-Anna's admonishments and encouragements, the hum of the onlookers, their whispers, and signs and wide-eyed exclamations, the shuffles and stretches of bodies too long constricted and contained – he tries to silence them all, to isolate the sound that is coming from the direction of the door. It is … knocking. Not exactly tentative, but inquisitive, asking, not demanding, to be answered. A rescuer then? Not police, too restrained, unentitled. Not the intruder, he imagines, too meek, too respectful. He allows the ambient racket to return and scans the room.

It seems the baby is finally coming. He remembers hearing – his mother, a talk show? – that this is perhaps the most dangerous time, that there is a potential for stuckness of movement or of breath. There is the potential for injury, for death, of baby, of mother. He thinks that they are all so tired, Miss most of all, that they are ready for reprieve, that they need help. For the second time that day, he decides to answer the knock. He decides to open the door. He will lift the window covering and ascertain the identity of the knocker before he opens the door, he will be cautious. But as he reaches the threshold, Miss bellows and bucks in a way both otherworldly and terrifying, and desperation animates him. He turns the knob and pulls the door toward him. He allows access.

It is not a rescuer, Mark immediately surmises. It is the intruder, and this is a surprise, yes, but the bigger surprise is the form the intruder has taken. He is one of them, young and untested, a boy Mark recognizes, but barely. The two young men stare at each other. Then there is another shout, not of the birthing variety, but of recognition, and then of vengeance. And Mark feels himself jostled and jounced from all sides; he had been holding the intruder's sleeve but feels his grip loosen as he is pulled this way and that. There is an attempt afoot to contain the intruder, but also to harm him, to punish him. One of the boys – Rahid? – has pinned his arms behind him, and Lauren is hitting him in the face, her blows haphazard. She is crying, red-faced. And then Mark trips and stumbles, loses sight of the centre of the fray. When he rights himself, he cannot see the intruder, who has been subsumed by the crowd, and he feels dizzy, unable to intervene, to do what needs doing. To show mercy and pull this boy, who is fundamentally like him, from the many-limbed mess of his classmates. But he is so tired, and so stuck. Why must it be him?

Then, from the far corner of the classroom, next to the towering filing cabinet, comes a figure, rushing and small, dark helmet of hair, denim jacket, grimy Converse. The figure windmills his way into the crowd, he elbows and kicks, he shouts stop, stop, stop, stop, stop. And to say a spell is broken would be too sentimental and would misrepresent the ways that humans find solace and solidarity in violence. The rupture is slower than that, more thready and strange. Lauren is the last to stop hitting, or trying to hit. Soraya and Brooke are holding her now. She is hyperventilating and Soraya is showing her how to breathe into her own cupped hands, to regulate her breathing. Mark cranes his head to see the identity of the guy who stopped it all. Who is it? Ah, it is Thanh, the one they all mocked for sleeping in the corner. So maybe they are in a fairy tale – and it is Thanh who has awakened to save them all from themselves.

FADUMA

Miss is so sweaty, her face so twisted and red, and in the middle of this last contraction she was staring at an empty space near her desk with a kind of confused rage in her eyes. It reminded me of Macbeth in the scene where dead Banquo shows up – bet she'd be happy to hear that. I wonder if sometimes giving birth causes brain damage. I squeeze her hand harder to put her in touch with reality. Then there's all this yelling from over near the door and I see Mark grabbing someone and I think, Finally, they sent help. But actually, it's not help. It's not even someone from our class. It's the intruder! A skinny white boy who could be good-looking if he did something with his hair. Then Mark and the intruder are lost in a crowd and I think: Not helpful. Really not helpful. A shouting crowd, a kicking crowd. WTF.

I feel Miss's weight stiffen against me. Another one coming.

I look toward Ryan, who is still timing, still manning his post. He looks back at me, nods.

When the contraction passes, I turn my attention back to Mark, back to the scene at the door. The crowd has dispersed; how? I scan and spot the white boy, who just looks sad, slumped up against a desk. His eyes are closed. There is a long red gash on one side of his cheek. Someone has tied his hands behind his back with white wire – earbud cords? Mark has eyes on him, but he looks like he's a little bit sorry for the prisoner. Is this really why we're stuck here? This little shit? He doesn't even look like he could pick up a gun. Allah, give me strength. It's not even a good story to tell. The other kids just look tired and sad and kind of useless, but then I remember how they stretched out their hands to me, passed me coins, met my eye, when I had to venture out into the unknown. And I understand that they are my parking-lot people.

SAM

Oh, Ant. Remember when you took my flower of power and handed me yours, as if we were exchanging tokens of love? As if you trusted me completely when I had given you zero reason to. How could I hate someone so stupidly vulnerable? It was like you had rolled onto your back, your ridiculous limbs in the air, and shown me your soft, downy belly and balls. If there was part of me jonesing to kick you where it counted, I had the sense and shame to counter it, to see that you were for me, that you – weirdly – already loved me, and I would have no choice but to love you too.

SHAI-ANNA

I watched it happen when I could, the retribution. It came to me from the other side of the room like a dream on speed, or a dream shattered by the loopiness of birth time. But in the end, we didn't let it go down, not that way. We chose a different way. And now? I watch Mark pull the kid toward him, hard, so that for a second they hug and sway back and forth. I think they will fall ... Another fucking emergency to deal with. Over by the filing cabinet a group of girls are sobbing. Hysterical. I know where they have gone, I get it. But come on. Why give in to that? Here? Now?

I recognize the white kid from chemistry class. He's actually pretty cute – flop of dirty blond hair and smart-ass eyes. He's thin but looks like he runs or something. Not like he spends all day playing video games. Still, he's a shrimp next to Mark, who's a bit of a gym rat. Fine-looking but not my type. The kid tries shaking Mark off, which is weird since I'm pretty sure he wanted to be caught, to be caught and held. Thank you, Jesus, this ain't happening on the street. Mark would be cuffed and slammed to the floor in a second, if not worse. The optics of it, you know? Big, Black, do-rag, boxers riding high, jeans riding low. Next to white-boy clean.

'Settle down, boy,' Mark says. Makes me smile.

They look like they might kiss, nose to nose. Then Mark flips him around and hugs him from behind. Some dude standing nearby hands Mark some earbuds and they tie him up – wrap the wire tight around his wrists. The white kid has lost his fight. His eyes are closed. I feel Miss's hand on my arm.

'I need to push, Shai. Let me push.'

I wave to Faduma, who takes my place at Miss's head so I can check her progress. There is some shuffling and rearranging over near the bookcase, and when I look up again I see they have made the kid a little cell in the corner and someone is giving him some water. Mark is dabbing at his own forehead with a paper towel, then reaching out to dab at the kid's lip, which is split and bleeding, but not much. The kid is shaking a bit – he's cold or in shock. Whatever. Down at the south end, things are moving along and I can tell another contraction is coming because of Miss's breathing.

'You can push,' I say. 'It's time to push.'

MARIA

I don't know why I decide to leave my classroom refuge. I know it is not protocol and could put me, or other people, in danger, but I cannot keep waiting. I am not sure whether my intention is to search the school or attempt to sneak out – either option is ill-advised. I have no plan, only an aching determination to do *something*.

I am on the first floor near the office when I hear the screams. My first instinct is to run toward them. To save Anthony. Not that I think that it is him screaming or even that I am convinced he is causing the screams, only that he is somehow connected. Is he hurting himself? It seems likely. I cannot sketch the scenario in my mind; it will not come to me in pictures, only in strange sensations of dread. I feel my body's ancient emergency response kick into gear – the amygdala taking over, ordering adrenaline, kick-starting instincts perhaps better suited to the ancient wild than here, in this place and time. Except maybe not. Before I begin to consciously calm myself, I attempt to assess. Is it possible this energy – as OTT as it may be – might help me? There are no bears to wrestle or outrun, but there are escalating screams undulating down this empty hallway, and a boy – a child, really – I know to be in distress. I open the door and run toward the sounds, my strides long over the dull, institutional floor, my breaths quick and urgent. I find the source of the sounds in room 108, although I cannot see inside. The door is locked, the window covered with chart paper from the inside as per lockdown instruction. The screams are animal in nature, un-self-conscious, from a deep agonized place. A woman or a man's? I pound on the door. Pause. Then pound again. A boy opens it to me – his eyes frantic and hopeful.

'I thought you were a paramedic,' he says. 'Miss is having her baby.'

His words do not coalesce in my brain. The smell hits me first – it is metallic and somehow carnal and it seems to hang like steam over the assembled students. I am scanning the room. In one corner, a barricade of sorts has been built, desks upturned and leaned against each other in a wall. Anthony is sitting behind that wall, his head bowed forward. Is he hurt? He looks up as if sensing my concern, then meets my eyes, unsurprised. Resigned. I can tell my arrival has broken something – a compact of sorts – between these people. They are having trouble fitting me into their cosmology, are wondering at my purpose. Anthony blinks, then offers me a weak smile, which releases me to scan the rest of the room. Most students are still sitting, as per protocol, against the walls, but a few seem to be gathered kitty-corner to Anthony's lean-to – and it is from this corner that the inhuman – or deeply human – sounds are emanating. It is at this moment that the words of the boy at the door click into place.

Someone is giving birth.

I decide to approach. To offer help? Or to bear witness? I am unsure of my motivation, know only that I must be near, to see for myself what I have only been hearing.

I walk toward the teacher's desk. I want something, a bulwark to lean against. My bowels have loosened; I have to clench a bit to keep things in place. And my knees – they are not working as they should. But I need so badly to see. Is the baby coming? How can a baby be coming? Of course a baby can be coming. They arrive everywhere – in the middle of rice paddies, the back seats of cabs, birthing pools, narrow cots, bathroom floors. Stirrups or squats. This is not a crime scene or a disaster. Is it an emergency? What constitutes an emergency? Maybe not an emergency but an intensity, a sharpening of priorities. I place my palms on the surface of the desk. Gunmetal grey, cold to the touch. Breathe. I turn myself, like a periscope, toward the sound. There are rolls of brown paper towel littering the floor. I step over them. A pile of sweatshirts, some of them wet or bloodied. Two pump bottles of hand sanitizer, one upright, one lying on its side. And an uncanny tableau of humans. I notice the boy first. He is crouched low in a squat, his elbows butterflying out his knees. One of his hands is resting on the shoulder of the mother, who is propped up on the knees of another person, a pretty, large-eyed girl in a pink hijab. His other hand points toward the midwife, who is kneeling between the mother's bent legs and raised hips. The midwife, who appears to me more than human, larger than girl or woman, is muttering what seems at first like an incantation, but resolves itself into words I can understand. *That's it, Mumma, that's it. Use that, use it, don't let it break you, hold on to it. You can push, you must push.* They are all connected by breath and blood and touch; it is as if a current is moving through them. I watch as the mother is seized and released, as the midwife tenses and hisses in time with her. The boy looks suddenly pale, then physically takes hold of himself. The girl at the mother's head bows her own head in supplication. The midwife measures and assesses, her head bobbing up and down in this cleft of time.

BORN

SAM

The mother is a monstrous thing, four-limbed but many-tentacled. I feel her reaching herself out into the classroom, selfishly, with such ferocity – and with something beyond and despite freedom. Her vagina has expanded, redly, wetly, to allow for this new thing her body wants both to clutch and expel. Make room, make room. Room must be made. It is not so simple, the addition of souls. It is exactly so simple. I know this new one does not mean to push me aside. I know hers is a path that slips and slides and wills itself differently from my own. I want her here, like I know myself to fit poorly here, to be a fish out of water, out of my element, untoward, unused and improper, inappropriate. I am inappropriate when it comes to this earthly realm.

SHAI-ANNA

'Now I need you to push. Bear down. That's it, Miss. Bear down. I can see the head.' It's true. I can see it crowning. It shows itself, then retreats.

Miss is tired. It has not been a long labour. I want to tell her to buck the fuck up. We can't get stalled now. But I know this all depends on her believing she can do this. The contraction subsides and the head is swallowed back into its cave. And who can blame the poor child? It's cold out here. And bright. Most humans are grade-A assholes. But at least she's white. At least there's that. Here comes another one.

'Push, Miss, push.'

Faduma is holding tight to Miss's hands. She looks like she might vomit. I meet her eyes. *Nearly there, Faduma. Be strong.*

Miss clenches her teeth. They are ringed red with Gatorade so it looks as if her gums have been bleeding or she's been feasting on raw flesh. Alarming but fierce. She grunts long and deep, then releases this breath that's part sigh, part fuck y'all.

And the baby's head is out. I am cupping it in my hand. Dark hair swirled with blood and vernix, white and cheese-like.

'The head is out,' I say. 'Rest for a moment. More work to come.'

Faduma looks at me like I am magical. And it's true. This is magic. Mumma's voice. *No more nonsense. Look at what is in front of you, not those fairy tales in your head.*

The next contraction comes, and the shoulder, and then the other shoulder, and then like a fish the baby slides out, just like that, like all that hard work was a big joke on us.

The baby is quiet, eyes squinched shut, and for a second I am just so happy she is out I don't check. The room is quiet, save for an exhausted whimper that seems to be coming from both Miss and Faduma – like they are singing their tiredness, but barely. And the smell! Everyone looks dazed by it, hypnotized almost. I blink and for a moment I am back with my granmumma, with the puppies and the smell, always the smell – of blood, of life.

Only a couple of people are filming. I cut my eyes at them and their camera arms jerk backward, but they do not stop. It's like they can't stop.

'Shai?' comes Miss's voice. 'Shai, what's wrong?'

I grab a gym T-shirt from our pile and wipe gently at the eyes, push my finger between the sweet small lips and sweep the mouth. The baby opens her eyes and looks straight into me like she knows all my secrets and will hold them close forever.

Then she opens her mouth and says, 'Ehhhh.'

It is a forceful sound but does not sound like a cry, not exactly. But it is enough.

The whole room starts to clap and stamp, beating at the walls and floors and doors like there is nothing that can contain them.

'Let me see her,' says Miss. 'Let me see her.'

I pass the baby up over her belly with one hand, lifting the cord carefully with the other. Then I lay the babe on her chest, between her breasts.

ANTHONY

'I'm in a state of high shimmer,' Sam said. 'Don't let me down.'

And she was. Her edges were sparkling when she laughed. It was like a bunch of crystals on a chandelier in a very rich person's house had been blown on gently by a god. We were in the park at our spot. She was eating chips, salt and vinegar, sucking them clean like a medieval knight with a bone. The sky was navy blue fading to denim at the horizon – it made me feel clean and like maybe living in the city wasn't so bad after all.

We scrambled down to the ravine and Sam lay down in the mulchy leaves even though they were wet and we'd had to do these awkward leaps over what were essentially mud swamps.

'What the fuck are you doing?' I said.

'My god, Ant. Chill out. Sometimes you have to actually feel the earth you're walking on, you know, like with your whole being.'

'Holy shit, Sam. You are so extra.'

'Maybe. But you should try it.' She sat up a little to look at me, then grabbed my leg and pulled me down next to her. She picked up some shitty old leaves with candy wrappers mixed in and spread them over our legs. 'We're part of it, you know.' She rolled toward me, winked. 'Why, O Natiya-thorn, dost wither? Why does thy cow on me browse?'

'It's gross,' I said. 'It stinks.'

'Yeah, well. It's beautiful too. It's decay and death and human disgustingness. All of our garbagey cast-offs.'

She rolled on her side and turned my face toward hers. I thought she was going to kiss me and I wasn't sure how I felt about that.

'Ow,' she said. She pulled a rusted spoon out from under her butt and held it up in the air between us. 'Who do you think first came up with the idea of a spoon? I mean, it's only slightly more effective than fingers ... You know, I read that in China people dig up five-thousand-year-old pots all the time in their backyards. Just like NBD. Imagine! Five thousand years. Would you go back if you could?' She was twirling the spoon between her fingers.

She was amazing.

I would go anywhere with you is what I wanted to say, but how brainless would that be?

SAM

Here is what I know to be true: this world is so shoddily constructed. We have used the wrong foundation, then fitted it out with all the wrong struts and beams. It will shake and shatter when the right gust of righteousness, of meekness, or even joy comes along. But the people like us – whether we stay or go – will continue shining, Ant. It's not us who are broken. It's not us who deserve exile. The world is fucked up. We're just observing and holding on as best we can.

ELISE

Shai-Anna puts her in my arms. My head is still resting in Faduma's lap and we look down on the baby together. She is wrapped in Tyrone's hoodie, which is mostly clean although I notice a smear of blood along one of the sleeves. Cold water and salt, I think. Or is that for red wine? I will have to tell his mother.

'Oh, Miss,' Faduma says. 'She's alive.'

'Yes,' I say. The tears are streaming down my face. I let them keep coming. The baby still doesn't seem sure, though. Little guppy out of water, her lips *oom-pahing* away.

'You need to give her the breast,' says Shai-Anna. 'Stop staring and give her something to suck on.' She rolls her eyes. But she's smiling too. And maybe crying?

Faduma helps me move aside the curtain she has draped over me, then begins the awkward process of arranging it back over my shoulder and around my torso.

'It's okay,' I say. 'I think they'll be okay with this. Modesty's not really a thing for me right now. Sorry.'

Faduma nods and frowns, then smiles when she sees the baby latch and begin to suckle.

And then for a moment I will remember for the rest of my life and well, well beyond, we are all – me and the entirety of ENG4U1-03 – watching this baby at my breast, willing her to thrive. It is bigger than prayer, this wishing; it is louder than thrash metal.

SHAI-ANNA

It's crazy how much I want my mumma to be here beside me. To see what I have done. I think she would probably just nod and begin to clean up, sucking her teeth at the 'absolute disarray.' But still. I want her here so badly that something shifts in my gut and a space opens up inside my chest and I begin to cry. At first just tears, then the whole show – snot and sobs. I have to sit down and I can't stop shaking. Then I feel someone's arms around me in a locked circle. Adio? No, it is Ryan. His grip on me is surprisingly strong. I lean into him without meaning to.

'It's okay,' he says. 'You did it. It's over. There is a baby.'

I want to tell him that is not the reason I am crying, that there are other reasons that he couldn't possibly understand, but then I realize that for now, in this moment, he doesn't have to. And I let myself be held.

ANTHONY

The baby is out and one of the students has placed it on the teacher's breast where it is suckling like a little mottled pink pig. They have forgotten about me, which makes me glad. It means I can talk to Sam without drawing stares. Crazy white boy.

Crazy white boy, my ass, comes her voice, close in my ear. *Do you really want to be the star of another story that ends with the crazy white boy outed as vulnerable and misunderstood? Do you understand nothing of the appeal of disaster narratives? Where's your follow-through? Where's the body count?*

'At least there's blood,' I mutter. 'That's gotta count for something.'

Sam laughs. *It's motherfucking birth-blood! And you're still alive! You realize that we've actually ended up with an extra life here, right?*

I nod at her. She's making me smile with her know-it-all arithmetic.

And what's with all these people of colour playing midwives to a little white girl baby? She snorts, right up in my face, so I can feel her warm breath against my cheek. *We've come a long way, baby. But not fucking far enough.*

She's right as usual. And righteous as hell. Still. I lean to the left so I can see through the barricade. Miss is looking up at Shai-Anna, who seems to be advising her. I never really noticed Shai-Anna before. She just always looked angry and like she might kick me if she got the chance. But now she looks supreme and in charge. It's totally hot.

Of course she's hot, douche. For a smart dude, you are sometimes So. Fucking. Dim.

And that guy, the one who saved me, he's there too, like one of the Magi gathering to pay their respects, but all shy about the boobs.

And I can't say I blame him. This is some major *National Geographic*–type shit.

Will you miss me, Ant?

I feel Sam then, like smoke trapped in my lungs, like a basketball perched forever on the rim.

That is an impossible question to answer.

Of course it is. Purely rhetorical.

SAM

Holy fucking hell, that baby is beautiful. All scrunched up and red and slimy and fucking beautiful. Ant, there are things I wish I could tell you, things I can't tell you. I know you think you didn't save me. I know you think you failed me somehow. I know it will take you a long time to understand that you didn't. If I could ... You know how Hamlet Sr. couldn't tell Hamlet Jr. everything about where he was, even if he wanted to? All that 'I could a tale unfold' shit? I can't unfold my tale to you. It's too much my own story. But, Ant? You did save me. You saved me every single day.

ELISE

I think I see Nate being bundled into the classroom by a coterie of cops. He looks terrible, like he's been electrocuted and maybe has pinkeye. I hate him. I love him.

'Miss,' says Faduma. She is holding the desk scissors. 'Do you want me to … ?' Her eyes are wide with the responsibility.

'No,' I say. 'No.' Not because of Nate, who may or may not be capable, but because of me and her, the new one sprawled on my belly. We need a little more time, linked like sausages, something more urgent and enduring than love connecting us. Nate will reach us. Someone will saw or snip through the cord. It will happen, I understand that. But not now, not here, not yet.

MARIA

I sit next to Anthony, or as close as I can get, and I snake my arm through the desk legs and stacked textbooks, so that I can touch his ankle. He looks at me and raises his eyebrows.

'Hey,' he says.

'Hey,' I say.

The kids around us have stopped cheering but are still giddy with joy and relief. No one is watching Anthony. He doesn't need watching.

From the hallway comes the sound of running, heavy footfalls, a mob bearing down on us.

Anthony sucks in his breath. What will become of him?

I reach over and take his hand.

'Forgive me,' I whisper, and search his face for absolution.

His eyes fill with tears; he nods and jerks his chin toward the scene in the corner. We turn together to watch.

The kids crowd around the mother and baby, form a circle, another barricade of sorts. They are crouched or leaning or sprawled. Some of them have linked arms, others are stacked against each other in precarious Jenga-like formations. They are focused on their teacher in a way they seldom are, I imagine, in the lull of the day-to-day. Through the chinks in their wall and the hum of their tending, Anthony and I observe. What will happen next?

The baby wails.

And then the outside world breaks through. The room shakes with stomping, the air thickens with shouting and radio static. Anthony's grip on my hand tightens.

The men with guns must see the bloody rags first, the viscera and mess of so much hard work and deep caring.

I hear them radioing for an ambulance and barking orders framed as questions at the kids. They are searching for a culprit, a place to lay their blame. On a single boy? On the teachers and mothers? With their bodies and shouts, the snug protection of their uniforms, the dark shapes of their guns, they are asking the students to break their circle.

But no one stirs.

The students look to the baby for their next move.

FADUMA

Tell me.
    Who gets to decide what is a good story?
    Welcome, new human.

NOTES

Elise quotes liberally and sometimes not quite accurately from Shakespeare's works throughout the novel; all credit to the Bard.

The comic Elise refers to on page 62 ('I went into teaching because I've always loved crazy parents') is by Bruce Eric Kaplan.

On page 71, Anthony quotes the line 'Imagination is better than a sharp instrument.' It is from the poem 'Yes! No!' by Mary Oliver. He then refers to a line from a John Ashbery poem: 'As steam from a wet shingle, and I am happy once again.' It is from the poem 'The Skaters.'

The verse Samantha recites on page 129–30 are lines repeated by Bengali storytellers at the end of every story. This version is from *Folk-Tales of Bengal* by the Rev. Lal Behari Day, available online through Project Gutenberg.

ACKNOWLEDGEMENTS

Thank you:

The Canada Council for the Arts, the Ontario Arts Council, the Access Copyright Foundation through the Saskatchewan Arts Council, and the Toronto Arts Council, for financial support. This book-writing gig is a long, uneven haul; money helps.

The incredible Toronto Public Library system, which has granted me, and many others, the space to think and dream (and to access other people's thoughts and dreams).

Rob Pazzano, Ruth Brago, Hodan Ismail, Christina Giagilitsis, Monika Szily, and Kathy Donachie for injecting hope and humour into my day-to-day work in public alternative education.

My students past, present, and future – for embodying challenge, wit, and wisdom.

Margaret Gdyczynski, who gets the virtual and real-life stuff.

Kristin Sjaarda, for walks, talks, and photography.

For all sorts of sustenance: Kathryn Walsh Kuitenbrouwer, Nithya Vijayakumar, Stuart Ross, Alysa Hawkins, Izida Zorde, Joel Freeman, Sarah Henstra, Angie Hilts, Brenda Bucci, Chrissie Bel Urpeth, Peter Urpeth, Ruaraidh Urpeth, Peter Checketts, Andy Checketts, Anne Freeman, Bob Long, Sue Merrill, Rami Schandall, Amna Hussein, Camille Freeman, Lyla Birrell, Tracey Freeman, Patricia DiTillio, Kirsti Conway, Megan Wesley, Nancy Cregan, Christine

Fischer Guy, Jenn Shin, Sandy Steen, Lilian Chau, Catherine Bush, Barbara Berson, Amber Wilson, the Hiskett and Barclay clans.

Julia Zarankin and Hodan Ismail for their clever, compassionate suggestions for this story.

Peter Burnett and Leamington Books for an early reading of the novel and general literary bonhomie.

Natalie Olsen for *Born*'s beautiful cover design.

Alana Wilcox, publishing/editing stalwart and all around good egg; Crystal Sikma for graceful editorial guidance; James Lindsay for publicity wizardry; and the crew on the floor at Coach House who make good-looking books and look good doing it.

My mother, Jenny Birrell, for teaching me about survival.

My sister, Julie Birrell, comrade in writing and reading and teaching and mothering, and my heart's confidante.

My daughters, Maisie and Eleanor. You guys are annoying and irreplaceable. I love you.

My husband, Charles, who loves me because/despite.

Our dog, Angus, who does a little jive when I come through the door.

Heather Birrell is the author of the Gerald Lampert Memorial Award–winning poetry collection *Float and Scurry* and two story collections, *Mad Hope* (a *Globe and Mail* top fiction pick for 2012) and *I Know You Are But What Am I?* Heather's work has been honoured with the Journey Prize for short fiction, the Edna Staebler Award for creative non-fiction, and ARC *Magazine*'s Reader's Choice Award. She has been shortlisted for the K. M. Hunter Award and both National and Western Magazine Awards (Canada). Heather's essay about motherhood appeared in *The M Word,* an anthology that broadens the conversation about what mothering means today, and an essay about post-partum depression was a notable mention in *Best American Essays 2017*. Heather teaches at a small alternative high school in Toronto, where she lives with her mother, partner, two daughters, and a whoodle named Angus.

Typeset in Arno and Agrandir.

Printed at the Coach House on bpNichol Lane in Toronto, Ontario, on Zephyr Antique Laid paper, which was manufactured, acid-free, in Saint-Jérôme, Quebec, from second-growth forests. This book was printed with vegetable-based ink on a 1973 Heidelberg KORD offset litho press. Its pages were folded on a Baumfolder, gathered by hand, bound on a Sulby Auto-Minabinda, and trimmed on a Polar single-knife cutter.

Coach House is located in Toronto, which is on the traditional territory of many nations, including the Mississaugas of the Credit, the Anishnabeg, the Chippewa, the Haudenosaunee, and the Wendat peoples, and is now home to many diverse First Nations, Inuit, and Métis peoples. We acknowledge that Toronto is covered by Treaty 13 with the Mississaugas of the Credit. We are grateful to live and work on this land.

Edited by Alana Wilcox and Crystal Sikma
Cover design by Natalie Olsen, Kisscut Design
Interior design by Crystal Sikma
Author photo by Kristin Sjaarda

Coach House Books
80 bpNichol Lane
Toronto ON M5S 3J4
Canada

mail@chbooks.com
www.chbooks.com